The little Yew Tree Witch
Author & Illustrator
Victoria J Hunt

01/03/2021
©

The little Robin follows me where ever I may go
For Dad & Grandad

THE UNFORTUNATE EVENT OF A WILD CAT WHO CALLED HERSELF HESTIA 1204

The gentle valleys were covered in ancient woodland, wild animals roamed and foraged the endless countryside, hidden deep from the eyes of man, the wild lived only in fear of their natural hunter. A large and proud wild cat who called herself Hestia, prowled and hunted freely in her domain. One day Hestia would fall in with very bad company. In the darkest part of the forest a coven of witches lived and they adopted her one fateful day as their pet. Hestia would at first enjoy the mischief and the tours, the young witches would love to explore and as their magical powers grew so did their trickery and power. Hestia was so impressed, she forgot her freedom and life of ease and was soon a slave to their spells and plots. Hestia grew older and asked for a potion to make her stronger and maybe to live longer, she could see the witches did not age, with cackles and prods they gleefully agreed and poor Hestia was tricked and set in stone, a statue she stood for hundreds of years and one day she was found and placed gently upon a fine mantle piece in a Stately hall.

STOURTON HALL 1809

Octavia was the youngest of four her eldest brother Hugh had died before she was born, her Father would never except his tragic death and his bedroom and place at the table stilled remained as if he was just out on a walk and would soon return, she had two elder sisters Cecelia and Olivia. Octavia considered that she had the worse possible name in the world, her Father had just named her the month she was born October and from a very young age Octavia felt no more than an after thought, her Mother Beatrice had tragically died only hours after giving birth to her and her Father saddened beyond belief, would also she thought have preferred a boy, an heir to his banking empire and vast inheritance and a child to replace his lost son. From a young age Octavia called herself Avia and sought ways to entertain herself away from her Fathers disapproving eye, he was rarely in residence since their Mothers death, so the girls knew little of their Father other than he had a passion for antiquity. Their Grandfather had been a keen collector of Italian art and bought his ideas back to England, an Italian renaissance from the grand tour transformed the house and gardens. He had travelled through Europe, China, Japan, India and the America's each time bringing back fresh ideas in style, culture and cuisine. The huge stately home and stunning gardens became the envy of many wealthy land owners and many would seek invitations to the lavish dinner parties, only attended by the aristocracy and very wealthy. Avia's father had been left all of this empire, he had no appetite for any of it though since the loss of Beatrice his dear wife, he would leave the banking to others and pursue his love of archaeology and art collecting. Sadly poor Avia would not feel her Fathers love he could hardly look at her and as she grew, he avoided home more. For Avia unlike her sisters, she was a mirror image of her Mother. Avia's Father Lord Richard Hoare would from the day she was born spend most of his time in his study, in London or abroad, the children were left with the adoring Nanny and a host of governess's and servants, they did experience more freedom than most girls of that era, however they felt like they were orphan's at times in a huge stately home with empty rooms and endless corridors. Avia and her sister Olivia were still too young for the social scene and were kept supposedly hidden in the wing of the nursery. Cecelia would be the first being the eldest to be found a suitable husband, he would have to be from a wealthy family with a very good standing in society to reach her Fathers satisfaction. Olivia her middle sister had already in secret given her heart to a wealthy boy who lived not very far away in a very impressive Stately home just outside Bath, they had a huge deer park and although their gardens were nowhere near as impressive as Stourton, the grandeur was still imposing, the young lords name was Thomas Blaywayt, Avia doubted though he would stick around forever he was so young, even though Olivia was the cleverest girl he would probably ever meet. The three girls were incredibly different in both looks and personalities. Cecelia was fair with the greenest of eyes and small with a tiny frame, Olivia was taller and slim with light brown hair and greenish grey eyes, Avia was tall and skinny with the darkest of hair and eyes all were exquisitely striking. Cecelia loved books and spent hours in the library she would often talk about her favourite books and the characters, as if they were real, often she would discuss them with her governess as though they were sitting there in the same room. Avia loved it most when Cecelia read to her, her favourite story was about a little Princess who went to live in an orphanage and got rescued by her adoring Father who had been away in India. Avia thought she would like to go to India it sounded amazing with all the colours, spices, elephants and tigers. A guest had once said it was very hot and stuffy and far to crowded in the city, with a dreadful smell, he however complained the fish was to salty at lunch, so Octavia thought he was not worth his salt, even she knew salmon gravlax could not help but be salty. Avia's other sister Olivia was different she spent her life learning she could speak french perfectly and knew all sorts of things you could do with numbers, she would often strut around talking of how she would love to go and be a scholar in London, her boring friend Thomas was going to go to London like his Father to become a Lawyer, they were unbearable together and spent hours learning Latin and when the weather was very fine they would spend days on the swing just chatting and reading informative books to one another. Olivia was most definitely the favourite she could play the piano beautifully and sang like an angel, although Avia found it a little high pitched and often it would irritate her, so she would excuse herself with a headache, not that she had really ever had one, it was just that was how she had seen her Aunt escape a room in a very dramatic way, Avia had watched her intently and had her performance off to an art. Avia by far the wildest of the three loved the gardens, she would spend hours roaming and learning all about the trees and plants, she knew the name for nearly all of them on the estate, she was learning all about the flowers and how they like to be positioned, it seemed some were very fussy about full sun, shade or their soil and some preferred more water than others, they needed pruning and dead heading and all sorts of attention, there were bulbs and seeds that required different steps, topiary, hedging, climbers and creepers the list was endless, what she really wanted to learn though was how to take a cutting from a plant to grow another, this to Avia was the most fascinating of things. She loved the gardeners and thought them her friends, they were always happy to chat to her and showed her how to weed and plant. Sometimes she got to go back to Tomsk cottage on the estate his daughter was her age and called Lottie they would play in her little garden. Avia loved Lottie's cottage in the winter it was wonderfully cosy with a roaring fire in the one room they all lived in, you could smell the delicious bread cooking in the range, in the summer she loved the washing on the line and the way Lottie was aloud to take her toy outside and leave things lying around. Miss Bonneville the housekeeper was very strict about leaving things leaving around at the Hall, Lottie's Ma and Pa were warm and friendly they were always hugging Lottie and they played with her and listened to her. Lottie knew everything about her Ma and Pa and it seemed her Ma and Pa knew everything about everyone in the village and on the estate. Lottie's sister Lucy worked up at the Hall as a scullery maid, she was always kind and cheerful she had lovely long blond hair and blue eyes like her Ma and Lottie. Avia always thought it was funny how everyone came into the world a different shade, her sister Olivia had explained it was to do with your genes, something like if a bay horse and a bay horse have a foal it will most definitely be a bay with a slim chance it could be chestnut or a grey should one of its Grandparents have been one of those colours, it was all a little complicated and Avia had just pretended to understand, although she had put the theory to her thoughts and wondered if you could mix the colours up of flowers, when she asked Tomsk he had said that was possible with something called cross pollination, he had no time to show her though, it was very disappointing to Avia and she was not certain he knew how, however, this topic of interest would force her to the library on a cold and rainy day imprisoned by the bad weather. Nanny Maud forbid her to step a foot outside in case she caught a cold and died, this seemed a little dramatic to Avia, she did love her Nanny though, so didn't wish to upset her by dying and stayed indoors. The library was always a little stuffy it was kept warm by the fire and huge drapes kept out the draft and candles lit the room for reading. Avia would select a book with difficulty, flower and garden books always won in the end, she would then go and sit on the floor in-between the drapes and the enormous windows that stretched from the ceiling to the floor, this way she could see the pictures and read some of the words and she was almost outside, but not, so she would not catch her death. Avia would often though end up just starring out of the window day dreaming about being outside in the gardens.

CAPABILITY BROWN

It was the year 1809 the date was October the tenth, Avia was nine years old, her Father was away in London he sent her a charming pottery doll with real hair its features were so delicate and fabrics so pretty, it came in an extravagant box wrapped in pretty ribbons, although Avia was not keen on dolls she appreciated it was special. Avia enjoyed the freedom of her Birthday with her Fathers absence, her sisters and Nanny Maud made a huge fuss of her they played games and ate so much, Avia felt a little giddy. Cecilia gave her a special brush with a pearl back, she had found it glistening in amongst their Grandmother's belongings and she was sure her Grandmother would love Avia to have the soft pretty brush, it was of no use to Grandmother in heaven, the angels would be brushing her flowing locks. Avia's favourite present though was from Olivia and Thomas they gave her a book on landscape gardening, the book was beautifully bound in brown and gold leather with a marble effect on the front cover, it had painted illustrations by Repton, a then famous landscape gardener who had taken the place of the late Lancelot Capability Brown. Avia was so thrilled and thanked her sister and promised to write to Thomas and thank him for his kindness, Olivia then giggled, the only thing she liked was the wretched garden, so it seemed an obvious gift other than a shovel. Avia was not offended in the slightest and agreed she was obsessed and inspired by Capability Brown, Repton and her Great Grandfather Henry Hoare the magnificent, who created the garden that wrapped itself around the Hall like a beautifully oil painting, strolling around the gardens one truly felt you were in a master piece, with exotic plants and more established native ones gifting elaborate displays of superb colour and texture throughout

the year, the garden was designed around the beautifi
bridge that gently arched over its tranquil waters, tha. ...
wards the tiny blossom island and shores of pretty paths, temples
and a grotto all embellished the gardens wonder, Avia's favourite
though was always the little gothic cottage that sat tucked away,
historically it was once completely hidden deep in the ancient
woods, before the gardens time, locals said it belonged to a
witches coven, who ran wild in the woods stealing children and
what ever else they could. Avia wasn't afraid though and was rather more drawn to its history fascinated by folk tales. Later on
Nanny Maud had given her a drawing book with a set of water colours and brushes, she had ordered them with Miss Bonnevillle's
permission and the houses purse. Avia thought this was the best
birthday ever, now she could really become a landscape gardener
like her Grandfather, she wanted to travel the world and create the
most spectacular gardens people would flock for miles to see. She
thanked her family and kissed them each in turn. Nanny Maud
was sat in the corner as always quietly watching and smiling, she
embraced Avia then scuttled back to her duties. Avia often
thought Nanny Maud was like a little mouse, when you entered a
room she was not really visible so timid and small with dowdy col-
ouring, Avia would watch her and she would sniff the air twitch-
ing and sometimes she would raise her little hands up together
and rest them perched under her chin, she was never loud or bossy
but gentle and kind, instead of chastising the girls, she would invent away of a problem being solved, smocks and old boots for
Avia with a bowl of hot water and a scrubbing brush on standby,
for Cecilia a piece of slate and chalk was put on her mantle with
the things she had to do, mainly lessons and entertainment of visitors, her books would be put by the slate with a pocket watch
should she forget things. For Olivia it was simple she trained her
to count to ten and look around a room before she spoke, avoiding
unnecessary arguments and hurtful remarks she could not easily
withdraw. Nanny Maud was totally trust worthy they could tell
her anything and she would find them the best solution to resolve
their quandary, or she would find away for them to do what they

wanted in a correct and more timely manner. Nanny Maud noticed everything and said very little herself, her mission was in no doubt that the Stourton girls would be content and well cared for in their extraordinarily affluent abandoned circumstances.

AGNES OF STOURTON CASTLE 1809

Avia was in the garden reflecting on how content she felt at this moment in time, her sisters were being kind, her Father away and the house had an easy feel to it, the butlers whistled and maids sang. The dawn had bought a crisp morning with sunshine and mild air, Avia munched on a Bath Bun she had pinched whilst running through the kitchens, cook Anna had waved a finger at her with a huge grin. In the garden she saw Tomsk and the new assistant Jack, Tomsk was showing him how to mulch the flower beds up near the house to protect them from the winter, stop the weeds and keep the moisture in. Jack happily whistled away while working and seemed very enthusiastic, he had a broad open smile and thick curly blond hair and blue eyes, it turned out he was a cousin of Lottie's. Avia instantly liked Jack she did not introduce herself though and just acknowledge him with a faint polite smile, Jack returned the gesture and politely, said morning Miss Octavia, a little to sharply Avia bit his tongue off, insisting she was Avia, Jack look hurt and mumbled an apology, he carried on with his mulching and Avia stomped off feeling bad for being so snappy. She took the path down by the lake and wound her way up and down in the trees, patting their trunks as though they were horse's being praised, some of the trees were huge with species from far and wide, she loved the big red cedar and stood starring up into the abyss of its never ending branches wondering if they reached to another world. Avia ran along the path and ran up and down the steps to the Temple of Flora she swung around the pillars, had a little polite chat with a statue and then carried on, passing over the stone bridge hailing some bun crumbs to the ducks, Avia dangerously hung over the stone balustrades looking intently into the shallow water, to see if she could spot a fish, on cue for their performance of the day a little shoal of silver Dace danced past, then darted below into the weeds. Avia doubled back on herself and soon reached the Gothic cottage. The cottage had only recently been added to the garden once hidden deep in the woods, the path know swept passed it and the surrounding trees had been felled, the cottage had had a gothic style window added with a carved stone bench, and the roof was all re-thatched. Avia loved the cottage and was thrilled that Tomsk had allocated Avia her a piece of land near to it. Tomsk had pegged out with string her area where she was able to design her garden. Avia kept her tools and baskets in the cottage and set to work straight away, her basket was full of pegs that she started to place in areas of the ground, she had a picture in her head and on the next rainy day she would spend her time planning, sketching and painting her design. Avia drew her attention to the huge yew tree that stood so proudly, she wondered how many years it had lived and how many wonders it had seen, Avia wished a tree could talk, the bright red berries on the tree were out, they were very poisonous and messy when they fell to the floor, the birds did a good job of eating them though, the yew tree roots were a problem nothing would grow, Avia had an idea though a stream flowed from a little spring not far away at the back of the cottage, she intended to make a pond that would add charm to the little cottage, as she looked at the roots she noticed something shiny in the soil just poking out she scraped away the soil and beneath was a little pendant on a chain, charmed by it she put in her pocket to study later, Avia turned her attention back to her job, she would need help however she started to dig a small trench from the tree towards the stream it was hard going, she moved her spade and started to try from a different starting point, Avia sang an old Indian poem she had learnt, while she busily dug, Avia made some progress and as she dug harder she found the earth surprisingly gave way, giving up a cavern that lay beneath the shallow surface, there were the remnants of what looked like hinges and a wooden box painted with strange markings, the box had what looked liked leather bound books and little clay pots lay strewn about the rocks, something shiny caught Avia's eye in the subtle October sun it glistened, Avia lay on the floor afraid to tread in the cavern should it disappear from her feet, she could not reach so with a stick she carefully prodded around, she tried to flick the item towards her, eventually she hooped the small chain onto her stick it dangled precariously, skilfully though Avia manage to balance it to the edge and firmly in her grasp, as she clutched her second find of treasure, Avia heard a voice of concern from behind her, a stumbling voice asked her if she was ok and needed help, Avia turned to see Jack, she laughed at herself and explained herself, whilst quickly popping the shiny jewellery into her pocket, Jack helped her up and said he would be happy to help on his day off, Avia said he would do no such thing she would instead ask Tomsk to lend his apprentice once or twice a week. Jack and Avia walked back towards the house busily chatting about the plants and trees around them, Jack was impressed by her knowledge and Avia suitably impressed by his knowledge of birds and how he was able to recognise each song bird, they lingered by the Hall still chatting and giggling, Miss Bonneville the housekeepers stern presence by the door prompted Avia to say goodbye. Avia ran up to the nursery wing and into her bedroom, she quickly washed herself off in the warm soapy water in the bowl left by the maid and changed her over dress, Avia carefully hid the necklace and bracelet in her box under the bed and ran down to dinner, she joined her sisters as though nothing had happened her rosy cheeks and glistening eyes gave no doubt that she was up to something though. Luckily the conversation concentrated on Olivia who was favoured with an invitation, she had been invited to Thomas's house by his sister Edwina, for a game of lawn tennis, followed by afternoon tea and an evening dinner party, she would stay over night. They were sending their own carriage to collect her the next day with Thomas as the journey was long. Lucy the maid would go with her and everyone seemed very excited by this event, it was as though she had been proposed to. Avia kept her sharp tongue unlike her sister would have, she would often keep her bad thoughts to herself and she was still gloating from her wonderful and curious day. She could hardly wait to be excused from the table and ran straight to her room saying she felt exhausted and feared a mild headache. Avia closed her room door and ran to the box under her bed she ran the chain through her hands and studied the pendent, it was so shiny Avia knew it was not a precious stone, even in her short life she had seen diamonds, emeralds, sapphires and rubies in her late mothers jewellery collection, that had been carefully hidden by her sisters, as their Father seemed to have lost all sense of value. This stone was clear yet cloudy it had a strange blue glow when you held it up to the light, its chain was small so most probably a child's. The other chain was a bracelet with little metal charms attached she could hardly make out what they were. Avia slept heavily that night she had strange dreams, she was by the yew tree but everything was different, weird looking people gathered they wore strange clothes and chanted in words she didn't recognise, she could see fire and dancing and then she woke in a cold sweat, her bedroom window was open banging in the wind, Avia cried out scared and Nanny Maud was soon there, she closed the window and sang a soothing little song whilst stroking her forehead lulling her back to sleep. When Avia woke the next morning feeling tired the pendent and bracelet were still clutched in her hand, she quickly hid them in her box, washed and dressed into the clothes laid out for her, Nanny Maud had had the local seamstress make several long smocks for her to put over her pretty dress's so she would not constantly ruin them with her love of gardening. Avia ran down the long corridor and the huge wide staircase that turned in different directions and finally swept into the hall, portraits and stunning landscapes filled the walls, side and centre tables in solid limestone were positioned in the hall with huge patterned vases filled with fresh flowers from the gardens green houses, the marble floor stretch endlessly through joining rooms for entertaining, with chandeliers that glistened in the morning sun streaming through the grand windows, Avia's feet patted on the shiny cold marble as she ran into the breakfast room where a huge comfortable rug nearly covered the waxy floor boards. Avia as always late sat with her sister who sipped coffee and looked at the daily newspaper ordered daily for their absent father, the girls had become accustom to reading about the wider world, ladies were not supposed to worry themselves or read such things, it seemed silly to let the papers go straight to the servants and then the fire, so Cecelia and particularly Olivia enjoyed discussing all sorts of topics. Avia still struggled with her reading she however enjoyed the pictures that Cecelia passed to her explaining in brief the story to the picture, missing out any harsh facts. Cecelia felt it her duty to Mother her little sister being five years older, she had had her Mama so remembered her gentle way's, pretty face and sweet smell, she still missed her dreadfully and would often just sit in her Mama's old bedroom, you could still faintly smell her perfume, Cecelia would chat to her as though she was sat next to her, she would tell all about everything, she would even ask her questions and decide upon her Mama's judgement with her own reply, agreeing totally; that was a good idea. The picture Cecelia showed Avia that morning was of a very smart French gentleman in and amazing uniform he was called General Pierre Dupont and was reportedly in prison after leading and being defeated in Baylan in the Peninsular war that had started in May 1808. Olivia commented he will no doubt not look so smart and handsome now, Avia didn't really understand, she thought the picture was very interesting, especially his medal it was very elaborate and had intricate carvings of crosses, set around a medallion a little like her pendent stone it had a faint picture of an angel holding what looked like an anchor, Cecilia said it was the Order Of Saint Michael, how she knew that was a complete mystery to Avia. The conversation then turned to Olivia's trip to stay with Thomas and his sister Edwina, Olivia was so excited she could barely eat her breakfast and just moved her toast around the plate; she had her favourite green dress on, Avia thought she looked wonderful and complimented her, Olivia surprised by her little sister rare observance of someones appearance made her blush and giggle. Avia was not really interested in how she looked, it was an effort to brush her hair, Martha the maid always struggled with her wriggling and protesting at the sight of a brush. Avia excused herself, after eating her bun and drinking two hot chocolate's, she quickly wished her sister a wonderful time and disappeared as quickly as possible, Avia then raced down the narrow hall and stairs that led to the kitchens, at the bottom she bumped into Arthur the oldest butler in the world, who cursed her speed under his breath then shouted after her, Miss Octavia be more careful you best not fall, Avia chanted back ,sorry and my names Avia. She took a huge red apple from the larder and bolted out of the servants entrance into the gardens. The air felt cooler than yesterday the autumn sun still shone though, Avia's first job was to find Tomsk so she headed for the kitchen garden, he would normally smoke his tobacco with a drink at this time in the old glass house, a huge new one had know been built producing an abundance of creamy white peaches they tasted so delicious and were used for jams and puddings, Avia licked her lips at the thought of peach jam, sure enough Tomsk stood with Otto and Jack, Jack was crouched on the floor petting Otto's dog a brindle bullmastiff called Benny, Otto was the Game Keeper, Avia was a little scared of him and Benny until she got to know them better, Benny was so friendly he just looked vicious, Otto said they both needed to look "real meanuns" to keep the poachers away. They had deer, pheasant and grouse to protect for his lordship, Avia hated the hunts when they came, she strangely would have preferred them to be poached at least then they went to the hungry, Avia couldn't understand why some had to be so poor and do without so much, when they had more than enough, when she was older she hoped she could change lots of things. Avia went up to Tomsk when he had finished his smoke, out of respect, he cheerfully bid her good morning, Jack immediately got up and grinned at her, while Otto eyed her cautiously, Avia asked straight away if she could have Jack to help her build her garden, Tomsk at first tutted, he said one day a week and no more, this Avia accepted happily knowing full well with the winter dragging its heels Jack would soon have less to do and Avia could pinch him more regularly. Avia skipped off with glee towards the Gothic cottage and her new garden, the trench with it's cavernous hole lay empty, she decided to wait for Jack to help her dig, Avia was just about to start pegging out her idea again, when she noticed something strange the little clay pots she had seen in the cavern, were now neatly placed by the yew tree and even more strangely they were washed out and shiny like they were new. Avia wondered if maybe Jack had done this although wondered why ever on this earth he would. Deciding to ignore the pots she continued to work Avia always forgot the rest of the world when gardening and time passed with such speed, the little Robin followed her with curiosity as she dug here and there, establishing planting places, she would have to wait until the spring to plant most things, Tomsk had said she could plant out her hedging though and she had already marked where the fritillary bulbs were to be planted. Avia had a very strange feeling though and felt all morning as though she was being watched, she began to feel a little uneasy so decided to walk back up to the hall and have her lunch; without being late for a change, still as she walked she had the eerie feeling of someone watching her, yet every time she turned there was no one to be seen, she listened hard and heard no footsteps, as she got closer to the hall she felt the presence was gone, after lunch she would go and find Jack and ask him about the pots, maybe some local kid was playing tricks on her, Avia however could not shake the feeling she had company in the garden. A few hours later Avia found Jack by the temple it was a steep climb so Avia was a little breathless by the time she reached the top, the views from the temple were amazing of the lake and gardens, Avia loved the temple and its statues that stood proudly around the building under the arches, it was named the Temple of Apollo dedicated to the sun god and true to its form it was golden, in stunning lime stone and sunshine. Jack was busy mulching the borders around the temple, Avia called him and he came grinning over to her, Avia reached into her pocket and threw him a large freshly baked bun, they both sat on the steps munching the stolen buns, Jack was a little confused when she asked about the pots and it was crystal clear to Avia that he hadn't even been near the cottage or yew tree, Jack was a little concerned and said he would finish up quickly and come and have a look with her, Avia helped spread the mulch while Jack shovelled it on from the wheel barrow they were soon finished, Avia then got in the wheelbarrow and laughing hysterically Jack pushed it down the bumpy cobbled path, while Avia pretended she was rowing with the shovel, they left the wheel barrow at the bottom and raced to the yew tree and the cottage, when they arrived just as before, by the yew tree stood six shinny pots, only this time it was even stranger two pots were full of a yellow liquid, Avia was worried Jack would think she was mad so did not mention this extra phenomenon, Avia was now really spooked. They both walked all around the perimeter of the cottage and up into the woods but could see no sign of anything, so Avia regrettable excused Jack so he would not get into trouble and tried to concentrate on preparing the earth for her hedges, every so often she would glance over at the pots mystified, she went over to them and took a closer look at the potion, it smelt strange she carefully put it back as she did she saw something out of the corner off her eye, Avia gasped her throat tightened and she felt scared, she was however rooted to the spot. Sat on the yew tree branch was a girl, she wore a beautiful blue dress with delicate white flowers, her hair was shiny black and she wore strange jewels, she looked around the same age as Avia. Avia stumbled to find words and bravely stuttered a demand of who her trespasser was. The girl quietly presented herself as Agnes of Stourton, when asked her age she was unsure, Agnes only gave the year fourteen hundred and eight, Avia gasped, gracious as she thought to herself this cannot be true it must be a dream, Avia felt wobbly and her head went all fuzzy. The next thing that Avia knew was she was waking up in the parlour with everyone flapping around her. Avia had fainted as she came around she felt very strange, everything was a blur she could hear Nanny Maud's voice saying she's coming around. Avia was taken to bed and given broth and sweet tea, Nanny Maud hardly left her side, her sister popped her head around often to check she was ok. Avia was very cautious of how to explain her fainting, the truth was absurd and if Nanny Maud heard her account she would never let her out again, luckily no one asked her questions until the following morning, Avia by this time had come up with a story it was simple she had felt unwell that morning and not eaten hardly anything, her story was accepted and she was made to stay in bed for the next few days, Avia was strangely happy to do so, unsure quite how to accept that what she remembered was true.

STOURTON CASTLE 1408

Stourton Castle was huge its turrets reached to the sky and huge thick walls held endless courts and inner halls, with elaborate rooms warmed by massive open fires, fur rugs lay on stone floors with huge pieces of furniture carved in oak scattered around, armour, swords and tapestry decorated the walls and placed proudly on beams stags heads with antlers gazed over the halls, outside huge courtyards stretched out, nearest to the castle were places of entertainment and seating, the arches lead to stable stalls, filled with sweet smelling hay and the sound of neighs and stamping hooves, an army of horses stood in wait of action or dozed tired from their earlier pursuits, the grounds stretch for miles, filled with ancient forests full of deer and other game, ponds and streams dwindled hidden in the canopies of trees. Lord Stourton of the castle owned the land, farms and villages all around for miles, his serfs had to pay him taxes and work for him farming the land, poaching was forbidden and a death sentence of hanging was carried out if caught, life for his tenants was hard a bad year of weather could see many of them starve, while the Lord and his family lived in luxury in the castle with tables laden with food, fires roaring and lavish furs to keep them warm, serfs of the castle were badly treated, although they were treated better than many in the land, their Lord was only doing what was expected of him, he had a kind heart though and showed some thought for his people, they could feed on the left overs and stay warm by embers, they were able to wear discarded furs and young children were free to roam, the servants treasured their jobs knowing they would not starve or freeze to death. The Lord had an army of knights with powerful horses, he would send his armies out to fight for King George, the knights were skilled swords men and took no prisoners, The King paid handsomely for his service and with the war still raging against France, they were never short of work or money. The year was 1408 it was a cold October and the day that a market was held within the castle walls, the stalls had a large array of farm produce, some sold hot pastries and mead served in lead tankers, others had rustic clothing and tools, the market bustled with carts, horses and people, fire pits roared and the peasants gathered to keep warm the market would go on late, games and fights would break out this would happen every sixth day after the Sabbath. Every sinner could then pray for forgiveness from God in church the following day and then rest if permitted. The peasants nearly all serfs to the Lord knew each other well, they were tied to the land and not permitted to leave, they all had their complaints and arguments, generally though they looked out for each other, a few were freemen and not tied to the castle, these were mainly the stonemasons and carpenters they travelled for work and would know folk as they often came back to the same place's for employment and had family scattered around. When someone completely new pitched up at the market though they were suspicious and not so friendly. Agnes and her mother, Avoca had arrived at Stourton in the summer four years ago, they arrived on a warm sunny day pulling their rackety cart full of their meagre possessions. They wore matching cloaks and pointed hats in a deep blue died by woad leaves, this was not sensible as it offended many, they were poor and not worthy to wear such rich colours, Avoca though knew it created work as she was skilled with dying fabric, folk could not help but ask for a deep blue or red garment. Avoca's cauldron bounced along tied onto the cart with other pots, furs and wool. They had travelled far on foot keeping mainly to the deep ancient woods hidden by the dark woody paths, they would camp late and rise early as not to be found, Avoca ran from captured and torture by a sherif of the Kings own, who believed her to be a black witch who had murdered his brother. Avoca was in truth a white witch she could heal with her potions and chants. The sherif was nasty and he had a personal vengeance, he sought out any who resembled a witch on his hunt, with no trial he would have them burnt at the stake, he became known and people were afraid and would quickly persecute anyone to save their own skin. Avoca and Agnes were lucky to escape and prayed to find somewhere less suspicious, were their skills could still be considered useful. When they stumbled upon Stourton they felt blessed the village folk were cautious, they however felt more gentle, the Lord who ruled the lands would soon find the healing powers by Avoca to be beneficial, she was to take a small stone hovel deep in the wood not far from the castle, there she had all the ingredients and utensils she needed to make her potions, ointments, powders and dye, Avoca and Agnes would set up a stall at the market every day before the Sabbath and to avoid persecution attended the church alongside the other peasants. On that cold October late morning Agnes and Avoca trundled into the market place within the castle walls, as always they went to the same spot at the end a little away from the other stalls, although they had not encounter any animosity they preferred to keep themselves to themselves and others seemed happy with their quiet presence, many had begun to trust Avoca and took her potions for ailments and since she had saved the life of little Tilly Feld from the sweating sickness, word had gone around and people treated her with gratitude. The morning felt uneasy to Avoca she was skittish and alert to everything, she had discussed with Agnes that maybe it was because it was the eve of Samhain and the fires would be lit to ward of evil spirits at dark, Avoca herself would pray to her ancestor on this eve in a stone circle she made surrounded by candles and herbs, it was a time Agnes loved as her dear friends would visit and she could sit outside all night and stare at the skies with them chatting of other times. Many stall holders were very busy that day and extra crowds gathered buying produce to celebrate the evening. Avoca was not happy though she twitched and sniffed the air like a fox tracking a rabbit, it became too much for her so they discretely packed up and left over the small side bridge no one used as it made the walk a massive detour to the village, Avoca was happy for this extra walk and to be away from the gathering crowds, as they entered the woods they could hear music starting to play and roars of laughter, they knew only to well this would turn to raucous bad behaviour later. Avoca settle herself down and held Agnes's hand firmly, she sang one of Agnes's favourite songs, pushing the rackety cart they disappeared into the depths of the woods. Avoca and Agnes reached their humble hovel in the woods still in the grounds of the castle, far away enough though from any one, only the odd game keeper would infrequently pass and a young farm lad, who she had found to be a friend, he bought her eggs and milk in exchange Avoca taught him how to dye the wool he bought from the fields, fallen from sheep, Avoca didn't normally like many Jeremiah though had a pure heart and was no trouble. That evening they both busied themselves with chores and began preparations for their evening, the stone circle was made and Avoca sprinkled her herb mixture as she chanted little rhymes as she named them rather than fixing spells. Agnes needed the doe adding sweet berries they had dried from the summer, she added mashed hazelnuts and then left it wrapped in a cloth by the fire, she placed the cauldron by the fire and went outside to help her Mother. The dark had come down quickly and the skies were clear lit up by the moon and stars, it was not long before the smell of smoke drifted through the air as the village and castle folk started to light their huge bonfires to ward off evil spirits. Many believed the spirits of the dead would travel, they would set a place at their tables for the loved and lost ones, who they invited in to join them in their feasting. Avoca though lit no bonfire she had no fear of any spirits and she invited no spirits to her table, instead she would greet her coven, they would talk long into the night and share knowledge, discoveries and spells. Agnes placed the doe on bay leaves in the dry cauldron she added sticks to the fire beneath turning her flattened doe until it cooked she then placed water and chopped potatoes and herbs in the huge pot unlike the others they would not feast on a sacrificed animal instead they would pray for the safety of the woodland creatures. Soon the others arrived magically just appearing from nowhere with only little pops of light flashing in the sky, the wondrous evening began. The five witches sat inside the stone circle eating the thick soup and flat bread that Agnes had made. Agnes played contently while listening and watching her Mothers friends, she was too young to be in the circle, Agnes loved to see her mother look so happy as she chatted in her own language, Agnes could understand some words though many were spoken too quickly. Each witch was different in appearance, all of them were beautiful and magical to Agnes, she loved Josina best, not only because she looked just like her own mother, she also had the sweetest smile and spoke as though she sang a song, her shiny dark hair and eyes glistened and she wore bright red clothes with pretty jewels, Josina always bought Agnes the prettiest dress's from far away and this years Samhain dress was exquisite finely decorated in delicate white flowers it was the most vivid blue in a luxurious fabric fit for a princess, Agnes loved it so much she danced and twirled admiring the beautiful flowing fabric, she was complimented by the others even funny Lettice, Lettice made Agnes laugh she had funny freckles and curly red hair, she wore many dress's in different colours all at once to hide her growing physic from an abundance of foraged and stolen food, she teased everyone with her drawl and at times was quite rude chattering through her wobbly teeth, Avoca had told Agnes she was ex-tremely old and was born into a viking family hence her rudimen-tal ways. Parnell and Wilmot admired her new attire and for Agnes this was indeed a triumph, for they were so beautiful and she had always looked at them both in awe, they were identical twins both fair and so pale they shone like diamonds, both appeared shy and quiet and each spoke for the other, they were practically one person in two bodies, Avoca had told Agnes they were the most powerful witches known on this earth, despite their demure and innocent appearance and soft gentle mannerisms. The evening continued as normal with laughter and chatter, until it took a more serious note, Agnes was an observant child and she understood from peoples tone of voice and expressions if there was any concern, that night normally filled with joy seemed to be taking a more somber turn. The conversation grew colder and quieter and the witches huddled closer. Agnes knew trouble was on its way, she stopped her play and went inside to the warmth of the fire lying down in front of the flickering flames she pulled a hessian blanket around herself and drifted off to sleep. Agnes did not sleep by choice the spell had already begun to weave its magic. Josina her mother's dearest friend came with grave news she had seen a vivid prediction, many of her gifts or curses she was never sure which. Terrified she had seen a vision of a priest, a sherif and crowd and on the stake with fire she saw Avoca and Agnes, Josina knew a witch hunt was upon them and they did not have long. Avoca had to leave with Josina that night they would take everything and hide what they could not take. To Avoca's horror this included Agnes she could not come she was to young and would die in the crossing of travel and time, Avoca begged her friends to find a way to take Agnes, they insisted though she would die, Parnell and Wilmot cast a spell so strong that little Agnes would not wake for hundreds of years, she would only wake if the words were spoken of an ancient Indian spell, her little sleeping body lay wrapped in hessian, with her favourite things in the chest, with henna they painted patterns upon the wood and carefully they gave sleeping Agnes a potion and there she would lie buried in a cavern under ground. Avoca planted a yew tree for protection and so she would find the burial cavern on her return, even if it took a hundred years. Wilmot had promised her she would be safe and when she woke little Agnes would be just the same, for now though she was frozen in time. With tears Avoca packed convincing herself she was doing the best thing, Josina had always looked after her and came back for her. Avoca could not shake the feeling that something was wrong, why would the witches coven not just take on the sherif and priest, she had no choice though and when she heard the sound of horns announcing someone of importance arriving at the castle she hastened, the other witches helped packing up making sure they left no trace in the stone hovel and they were gone, they vanished into the smoky skies taking their spiritual paths and portals to their world in different times and places, far from danger and far from Agnes.

SHERIF DASTIN AND THE PRIEST

Sherif Dastin had begun to quite enjoy his witch hunt, with a simmering rage over his brothers death, the search had given him the opportunity to seek out any wretched old hag he thought guilty of anything, he had gained momentum and had the company of a rather plump and vindictive priest, who sought to rid the Kings country of pagan beliefs and heretics, intrigued by Dastin's sorry story of his brother strange death, they became very dangerous and unpleasant traveling companions, each had the purse of the King and soldiers on horse back who had no empathy for others. Dastin had picked up a trail west from Winchester with many villages that seemed rife with paganism, after many cruel convictions he continued his journey, in search of more heathens and a castle that he had been requested to visit, the track was well trodden and took the fearsome group past an extraordinary spectacle of stones, they stood proudly in a circle on a plain of land that reached to the skies like the sea, the strange stones had a mystical eerie feel, the priest commented they had some ritualistic meaning, the way they were aligned with the moon and sun, they found unmarked graves and remnants of fires, the priest was nervous and pushed Dastin to move on, the night was the night when spirits and the devils own were said to travel and although his beliefs did not accept this, the priest had heard terrifying rumours of what happened to any found lingering to late at the stones on the Eve of All Hallows, Dastin agreed they should move on, he could tell by the footfall of the land that many visited the site of stones. They rode on delayed by the stone circle and did not arrive at Stourton Castle until very late, Dastin was there by invitation of the Lord who was inquisitive about his reasons for so many executions, he had sent a messenger conveying he had concern for his village and castle serfs, so he would like to be there when Dastin carried out his search of his land, The Lord of Stourton it seemed to Dastin was a very unusual man he wished to protect his people rather than punish them. Dastin reminded himself though he still sought his brothers murderer and no ground could be left unturned.

They were greeted with a little uncertainty, Lord Stourton had retired saying he would meet them in the morning and they were provided with a humble super and bed for the night, Dastin had hoped for a more lavish meal and chambers, he had heard amazing things about this castle stuck out in the middle of nowhere. After an uncomfortable nights sleep disturbed by screeches of owls and howling wolves, Dastin found himself sitting in a huge hall at a table with the Lord Stourton and many men and women all of different class, they talk openly and freely about the days work a head and discussed problems together. Dastin felt even more annoyed as he was ignored by the Lord, his ears pricked up when they talked of a sick child in the village and someone suggested they called on the healer in the woods to help, it was agreed and immediately a man was sent to find her. Dastin excused himself and followed without the Lords permission or notice. Dastin found no problem in following the young serf he had no suspicions and was happy to hang back and chat, the folk were so friendly, he answered no questions that Dastin asked though, just saying he didn't know the honest answer, frustrated Dastin followed listening to his constant babble about the birds and trees, knowledgeable as the young farmer called Jeremiah Feld was, Dastin had no appetite for such information and hastened him on, they finally arrived at the stone hovel and Jeremiah Feld called out if anyone was there, he tutted how strange and banged on the door, the door swung open showing the empty and abandoned room, Jeremiah scratched his head and excused himself running

as fast as he could back to the Lord, he needed to tell him the healing lady had gone. Dastin looked carefully for any trace he
searched in every nook and cranny but nothing could be found,
the only small clue was a piece of ripped red fabric on a branch behind the hovel, he studied the silky texture knowing it was no
poor hags fabric. Dastin placed the silk in his pocket a small trin-
ket for his trouble and he did not know why but felt sure this
wretched healing woman was his brothers murderer, he paced
back in anger to the castle to ask questions, Dastin would get no
sense from anyone as the serfs and Lord were more concerned
that they had lost the healing woman, she was clearly good at her
job and had the whole castle and village under her spell. Dastin
needed a plan these kind simple folk would not respond to his brutal questions, so he took council in private with the priest and they
agreed to walk into the village and see if they could help the young
girl. The day was pleasant and the mellow air was fresh, the sun
shone showing the stunning landscape, even Dastin had to remark on such a beautiful spot, he found Jeremiah and asked him
to take him to the village, offering him a small cloth purse full of
pennies, this to the serf was more than two years wages, Jeremiah
cautiously took the purse and hid it in his cloak, the walk was
brisk and the farmer Feld talked less and answered a couple of
questions about the missing healer, he probably felt with her disappearance he could do her no harm. Dastin was even more certain now he had his witch she fitted the description, he however
did not bother to discus this with farmer Feld. The village was
charming much like everything else and the folk friendly, never
had he seen so many pretty serfs, they all looked well fed and in
good health, he was taken to the cottage with the poorly girl,
Dastin had no care for the peasant and her family he and the priest
however made a good show of concern, the child had a bad fever
and the priest had seen this in many, he remembered that the
treatment most successful in London was simple enough, the patient would need to be dowsed regularly in cold water and given
cold stew stock and leaches to purify the blood, he prescribed this
with confidence and left. Dastin and the priest then looked around

the village, the mellow stone cottages were rustic and centred around a stone cross there was a large green area where sheep and chickens roamed, an oval duck pond was sheltered by a huge oak tree, children played under its huge canopy whilst some climbed up into the giant branches, carts came slowly along the rackety track, one full of straw for a cottage being thatched. Dastin and the priest watched the folk come and go there was no sign of the healing woman or any others a like, the priest noticed that most wore simple cross's made from woven dried grass's around there necks and often would make a sign of the cross on their chest, he watched several pray in front of the stone cross and lay flowers, the day was not even the sabbath, the priest and Dastin came away from the village feeling that the castle and village folk of Stourton were indeed God faring kind people. Dastin had no place here, the Lord of the castle was clearly ready to protect his serfs, it was maybe a blessing the healing lady as they had called her had gone for he had a feeling they would not have let her go without a fight. Dastin would find her somehow he thought, without word they left the castle to its carefree ways. Dastin would make his way with haste towards the coast he felt sure his witch would make for the sea and escape by voyage, he wondered if she knew he pursued her and thought to himself of course she did she was a witch. Dastin on the long ride, thought back to the stone circle up on the plain, something peculiar happened in that place, if only he had had more time to stay and watch.

The Lord Stourton was happy to hear that Dastin and the priest had gone he wanted no trouble and was pleased with his folk for causing none. He was frustrated though, for he felt sure that the healing lady in the woods had vanished because she had heard of Dastin's approach, he was an evil man and had caused wide spread fear on his conquest. Lord Stourton wished she had stayed he would have protected her and her sweet daughter, they had been a valuable asset to his community with superb healing powers, sadly the young child died in the village and as the Lord of Stourton suspected cures were not through prayers, but through good treatment and ointments, he feared though his healer had fled for good. Lord Stourton had his horse saddled and rode out to the village he visited the family to pay his respects and had food sent to them, he then rode on to clear his head and to look at his land, he had not had the freedom of late to ride through the ancient woods, he fell upon the stone hovel and dismounted to have look around the room as found by Jeremiah Feld it was empty, he could still smell the herbs scents though faintly on the air, he walked the perimeter and saw nothing other than a yew tree that had been freshly planted, in this part of the woods where only Oak, Elder and Beech grew, he however thought perhaps the healing lady sought to grow it for one of her potions, Lord Stourton filled his leather pouch with the fresh spring water that made a little stream and sat on the dry soft ground, it was so peaceful in the wood with not a soul around, he somehow felt though that he was watched was she was still here somewhere, he felt a strong presence of something, his thoughts were broken by young Jeremiah Feld who strolled along whistling, he jumped when he saw his Lord sat on the ground and asked him if he was well, Lord Stourton laughed and bid him to sit next to him, Jeremiah happily sat next to the Lord on the soft grass, he agreed it was a strange business with Dastin, the priest and the healing lady gone, he then took his opportunity to explain to the Lord Stourton how he had been paid handsomely by Dastin for information and as a guide, he explained he didn't know he was a dangerous man. The Lord understood and instead of taking the peasants purse, he asked him what he might do with such a small fortune, Jeremiah explained he would like to by some sheep and rent the glades of grassland in the wood, he said he had learnt from the healing lady how to dye the wool, he thought he could sell the wool at the market, the Lord was impressed and granted him free use of the land, he however would take a small share of his profits in return, they shook hands and parted ways. Jeremiah Feld felt he was a lucky man and he knew the healing lady or witch as he thought she was, had helped him somehow and if Jeremiah could have seen the future, he would have seen that this strange twist of fate with a witch or two would entangle his future generations again.

SAGE & FERN LEAVES

Avia had not been to the garden for a few days partly because she was told to have bed rest and partly because she felt quite scared. The sunshine shone brightly through her window though and she decided she would at least go to find Jack, so she wrapped herself up with more clothes than normal and called to Nanny Maud that she was taking a small walk, Nanny Maud came and fused over her, happy with her over dressing, she allowed her no more than an hour with no digging. Avia couldn't find Jack so walked towards the gothic cottage, she held the moon stone in her pocket rubbing it between her fingers. The garden to the cottage was as she had left it, the cottage though was not and was clearly been used, herbs and flowers hung from the beams and the smell of smoke lingered, a cooking pot lay washed and discarded drying in the sun. Avia turned on her heel to go back unsure wether or not she should report this to Otto. When she heard the voice again only this time it sounded a little more timid and scared, the stranger asked Avia if she would like some sage leaves, Avia replied curtly no she did not, then the girl Agnes appeared from behind the yew tree, she said in her strange voice that they were good for you when you were ill. This time Avia held her ground and decided if the stranger was going to hurt her, she would have done so when she was flat out on the ground, instead though she had put some leaves on her head, Jack had told Nanny Maud he had taken them off when he found her as they had a funny smell; Nanny Maud was concerned Avia had taken to putting leaves on her head and wondered if they were the reason for her fainting. Avia asked Agnes what they were and why she had put leaves on her head, so the girl replied they were fern and sage leaves soaked in peat water to keep her from over heating and stopping anything bad getting her, Avia hesitantly thanked her and asked the girl where she was from. Agnes clumsily explained in broken words she had lost her mother and everything was very strange, she couldn't see the castle and everything was different the deep woods had all turned to a lake with pretty trees and funny cottages and even the hovel was different, then she started to sob a little. Avia, felt sorry for the poor thing, what was she to do with her, Avia comforted her and told her she had to go, she would come back with some things for her after lunch. Avia rushed back to the house and joined her sisters at the lunch table, luckily everyone was in a quiet mood, Olivia was day dreaming, no doubt about Thomas and Cecelia was absorbed in a book, Avia ate as quickly as possible putting as much as she could in her pockets, she then returned to the gardens running along the high path that lead quickly down to the cottage she crossed over the bridge, normally she would have fed the ducks, her bread buns had a far more important job today though. Avia found Agnes sitting in the yew tree she climbed up and sat next to her passing her a bun, Agnes sniffed it and licked it then smiled, she liked the sweet sticky glaze and devoured the bun in seconds, Avia passed her another to munch. Avia asked Agnes the last thing she remembered and Agnes told her all about her mother Avoca and her coven describing each witch and saying how clever they all were, then she sobbed again because she truly was a little lost soul, Avia began to realise Agnes was a little witch. The more she told Avia of what she knew and how she had lived Avia was more and more certain she was a real witch, the mystery still remained how on Gods earth could she be here from four hundred years ago, Avia believed her completely that she was from another time, she couldn't possibly make such things up, Avia had to be really careful and protect her, she asked Agnes to promise not to tell anyone ever she was a witch's daughter, she was sure it was still possible she could be jailed or hung even. Avia studied Agnes she had long shiny black hair and huge almond shaped brown eyes, she was delicate and had the sweetest smile and a lovely way of expressing herself with dance like hand movements, Avia looked at her brace-lets and realised that the one she had found must belong to Agnes, Agnes said she could keep it as long as she wore it, she said it would ward of evil spirits and bad witches, Avia then asked her about the pendant, she timidly showed her with some reluctance, Avia did not wish to give it up, Agnes studied the necklace she bit on the stone and then held it to the sky, Agnes said it was precious and she was lucky to have one she said it was a moonstone and Avia should keep it on her at all times, Agnes said it was much more powerful than her bracelet and she smiled saying she felt happier that Avia would be safe, because she really wasn't sure if the witches would come back or if they had ever gone and Agnes started to sob a little again, she said she felt scared of the witches and her mother now. Avia agreed it wasn't the best thing to do to your daughter, bury her underground and leave her for hundreds of years alone in a box, she held Agnes's hand and just sat quietly with her for a while, she would have to sort something soon poor Agnes couldn't stay here all alone and scared, as Avia sat contem-plating their predicament, she became curious could her little witch actually perform sorcery, although now was not the time to ask her. Reluctantly Avia left her saying she would be back in the morning, she told Agnes to hide herself well and she would be fine.

AVOCA & THE FORT
OF CHITRAKUT
YEAR 1300

The night Avoca left her little Agnes behind was hard she left with Josina and travelled to another place and time, Avoca felt empty and missed her sweet little face and ways, it hurt to think of her lying asleep all alone in that box under the earth, Avoca prayed with all her powers she would be safe. As time passed Avoca started to enjoy her surroundings and she felt welcome in Josina's colourful world everyone spoke in her birth language and she enjoyed the dry climate and heat of the sun. She lived in a great fort called Chitrakut, she worked with Josina making healing potions and beauty remedies for the Queen Rani Padmini, she was the most beautiful person Avoca had ever seen, she loved her and was loyal to her service. Avoca felt safe and enjoyed a lavish life style she had once known before in the palace of her capture, every day she was fed with the other queens servants they had a rich diet of rice, vegetables, spices and exotic fruits, she had endless leisure time with others and was free to wander the lanes of the great fort, in the evening the women would bathe in the warm waters to cleanse their skins and dress in stunning silk outfits, they would perform dances and carry out ritualistic chants, then sleep in exquisitely decorated chambers. Avoca now understood why Josina always glowed, Avoca grew more beautiful herself, she gained knowledge from the elders and became an even more proficient witch, although Avoca was not named a witch or dankini, she was considered to have a profession in her potions and was needed in the fort. Avoca made friends and her life was rich and good, she thought less and less of Agnes and found it easier to try and forget her, one day she would go back for her, Josina said it was to dangerous to go back yet, so many things could go wrong, so they left Agnes while they thought what to do. Avoca and Josina were content and happily went about their business. Sometimes Josina would vanish for weeks, a few times Avoca travelled with her they would meet the other witches from their coven in a Chateau in France owned by a strange warlock called Fabian, Avoca enjoyed the pretty gardens and sweet kittens, the warlock though she was scared of, he reminded her to much of Dastin another warlock. The others would stay with the warlock Fabian deep into the night, Avoca though would hide in her room discouraged by Josina who said she would find the subjects of no interest. Avoca never really knew quite what Josina did on the occasions when Josina was away without her and Avoca never asked, Josina seemed very troubled from the last time she had been away and she was mumbling she was to late and shouldn't have left, she had visited the queen to tell her of her prediction, even this though could not stop the future, Josina was correct in her fear and failure to stop the war she predicted. On a fateful night only three years after they had arrived at the fort, they were woken by terrible noises and the smell of gun powder, others in their chamber started to stir and then an elder came in screaming for them to run, the fort was under siege with an evil plot against their King and Queen. Josina as always took control and they quickly packed all they could in the chaos, they heard shouts coming closer, Josina grabbed Avoca and they escaped narrowly as the door to their chambers was broken down, they ran in darkness down the tunnel used for bathing waters, it bought them to the river and from there they could escape to the mountains, the night was clear and very cold, Josina and Avoca dared not stop though or take flight in case they were seen, they could see so many soldiers marching towards the fort once their home, now a battle field of destruction, they could not believe that their wonderful life was destroyed. Josina would later learn that the fort was seized by Alluddin Khilji's vast army and that their king was gone and their beloved beautiful Queen had taken her own life, instead of facing the shame of her captor. The fort was said to be a place of horrors and Josina and Avoca were lucky to flee, Josina never forgave herself for not being there earlier to try and stop the plot, she grew angry inside as they hid deep in the forests on the mountain slopes, waiting for the next eve of Samhain.

WHERE TO KEEP A LITTLE WITCH

Avia had been looking after Agnes she had set the little cottage up as well as she could without to much suspicion, the grounds people thought she was just making a play house, she had instructed Agnes to hide if anyone came and together they would come up with a plan, she could not abandon poor Agnes nor could she tell anyone about her, if anyone was to find her they would send her straight to the poor house, Avia had heard from Lucy that the poor house was an awful place and dreadful things happened in those walls, that were supposed to offer sanctuary. Avia continued to steal food and clothes from the Hall, in return Agnes helped Avia to make her garden and slowly the two became the best of friends. Avia's little witch was clever with plants and roots she taught Avia how to mix a potion and soon the two of them became quite industrious making special plant food, Agnes would also practice her chanting of rhymes she had her mothers book hidden with her in the cavern, Agnes started with simple spells first, she realised that she was good at sorcery and discovered her talents, sharing her growing confidence with her trusted friend. Avia watched in amazement as Agnes moved things with her pointed finger without touch and how she made potions that did different things, her favourite was the healing spell, one day they found a rabbit in a trap, the poor things leg was a mess, within a week Agnes had completely healed the rabbit and with joy they watched it hop away. All this still did not solve their problem though Agnes could not hide in the cottage forever. One day Avia had a very clever idea, she had heard Jack saying that Rosy the scullery maid was leaving to marry a farmer. Agnes could work in the Hall then she would be safe and her and Avia could still be friends together, she just had to convince Agnes that she would enjoy working and somehow introduce her to Miss Bonneville. Avia explained to Agnes what a scullery maid did and Agnes liked the idea of working in the kitchen and washing pots and floors she would work on the tidy spell in the book, Avia and her laughed maybe she could do all her work with magic spells, Avia had to teach Agnes more modern ways of doing things and how she should speak some of her vocabulary was strange and a little rude, she also said she had to say she was older, eleven was the youngest they would employ someone at Stourton Hall. The next morning when Lucy was cleaning the fireplace, Avia asked Lucy all about how she got her job, Lucy had said she was just employed as they knew her family and employed most of them, she was helpful by telling Avia that strangers needed a reference. Avia now had a huge problem how would she get a reference for a witch who came from the year 1408. Avia needed help who ever could she trust though, Cecelia would be perfect she was so clever, it was too risky though, then she thought about Lucy's words, family, could she trust a servant to tell and never give her secret away. Later Avia walked around the lake trying to think, while Agnes played in the woods, she seemed to almost be flying from branch to branch, Avia was worried that they would not pull of this idea, so deep in her thoughts she didn't notice Jack come around the corner until he was upon her, Jack grinned and asked her for a penny for her thoughts, Avia jumped and laughed, Jack always made her happy and that was it, Jack, she could definitely trust Jack; Jack sensed she was up to something and presuming she was plotting for her garden, he enquired how it was going, Avia chatted away to him telling all her garden news and they walked to the Gothic cottage together, Jack was amazed she had done so much, he was even more amazed she had grown so much in the depths of winter, this became Avia's opportunity to mention her ward Agnes. Avia asked Jack to sit with her on the stone bench by the cottage window, first she asked him to swear on his life and Mothers to keep a secret, then she told him about Agnes, she had thought to leave the witch part out and only described her as different and someone who did experiments, however the more she said the more she sounded like a witch, Avia asked if he could maybe put a good word in for Agnes, by saying to the cook she was a long lost relative who needed work and lodgings. Agnes had been sat on the roof listening, Avia had told her to wait and not show herself yet, Agnes became so excited though, she had seen the boy called Jack in the gardens, he talked to the birds and sang lovely chants so she was sure they would be the best of friends, so Agnes scampered down and shocked poor Jack who went pale as a sheet, Avia held his hand and said it was fine she would not harm him, Agnes uncertain of his reaction quickly retreated behind the yew tree, Avia was suddenly not so sure this was a good idea, Jack looked most unwell, she called for Agnes to come back and introduce herself, hoping if she could show how sweet she could be he would like her, Jack though looked at the sun and excused himself saying it was time to go, he ran off calling back to Avia that he wouldn't tell, her secret was safe. Avia stomped her foot and called Agnes who arrived with her head down, Avia was cross with her, she remembered though Agnes was different so instead comforted her and said she was going to sneak her into the Hall for a sleep over tonight, her poor little witch would be warm and well fed. Agnes's eyes lit up and she danced for joy, Agnes hated being alone in the cottage at night.

JACK RUN RABBIT RUN

Jack walked away from Miss Octavia or Avia as she liked to be called as quickly as possible, once he was out of view he ran and like a hunted rabbit didn't stop running until he got home, his home was a small farm across the fields from the Hall, it had been in his family for centuries, his ancestors were once serfs to the lord of the castle, they had been sheep farmers who dyed their own wool and made well enough to build the farm house and buildings over the years. Wool was dyed now in enormous quantities by land owners with huge flocks of sheep. His older brother Bertie helped his Pa and they lived a reasonable life with a small heard of Devon cattle that grazed on the rich pasture land, they produced creamy milk that they made into cheese and butter for their own consumption and to sell at the market held every Saturday, they also sold eggs and chickens and anything else they could seasonally grow. Jack though had a real passion for the gardens and his Uncle Tomsk gave him the job and fare pay which helped his family through the harsh winters. When Jack walked into the farmhouse his Ma was busy churning the milk, Jack offered to help and his Ma took a well earned seat by the fire, the table was already laid for supper and the delicious smell of stew wafted through the room. Jacks Ma looked quizzically at her youngest son and ask why he had a furrowed brow, Jack asked where his Pa and Bertie were, as they were at stock market and not due back for a good hour, Jack felt safe to talk to his Ma, although he had sworn to Avia not to say anything, she had presented him with such a dilemma that he had no choice but to turn for help, he could not risk betraying the Hall, his family and other relatives were all dependent on the Hall for employment and homes, yet to not help Miss Avia was awful and to not help a witch could be dangerous, although Avia had never directly said Agnes was a witch, Jack knew straight away she was, what else could she be. Jacks Ma was the kindest and calmest person he had ever met and he trusted her with more than his life and so the tale was spun a little further, although that was where it would end. Belle, Jacks Ma listened carefully and was cautious not to comment until she had all the facts and when Jack had finished, Belle fluttered around the kitchen a little to calm her nerves, Jack waited patiently for her response. Belle took her son by the hand and whispered to Jack that the girl had to go she was a bad omen, Jack argued that she wasn't and said Miss Avia had taken it upon herself to care for the waif. Belle and Jack decided to sleep on it, the men were back and they both knew Pa and Bertie would go straight to the sherif, they would have Avia's witch captured and taken away, although Belle felt this was the best option, something in her heart and past made her think she should help. One thing was for certain though Jack must not lie for Miss Avia or the waif. The next morning Jack woke early he helped do some chores on the farm, then grabbed a hunk of cheese and bread from the kitchen table. Belle was sat mending some clothes she tiredly looked up at Jack, Jack felt sad he had caused her so much concern and wished he had kept his secret, as always though his blessed Ma knew what to do. Belle was friends still with the housekeeper Miss Bonneville and on their last meeting at the market, Miss Bonneville had told her how she sought a fine seamstress to design and make Cecilia's ball dresses, for her first season and new dresses for the younger girls, Belle thought this position far more appropriate than a scullery maid, Belle herself had worked up from a chamber maid to the ladies dresser so had many sewing skills herself, Belle began to tell Jack her plan, firstly she instructed that Jack, Avia and the little waif had to follow her plan exactly. Agnes was to learn to sew Belle knew she would be quick at this before she even met the girl, after all she suspected she was definitely a witch. Belle would secretly teach her all the skills she had been taught by the old seamstress at Stourton Hall. Belle herself made elegant gloves from fabric scraps. Belle would help the girl if she promised to use no witch craft and serve the Hall of Stourton instead with her fine needle work. The main part of Belle's plan was to be played in front of the whole village on market day. Agnes would arrive in her exotic clothes as Jack describe them with a basket of her fine sewing, she would linger at Belle's cheese stall at midday as that was the busiest time, Agnes would purchase a small piece of cheese whilst showing an enquiring Belle her fine work, the charade would be performed just as the housekeeper Miss Bonneville as always came to order the Halls cheese, milk and butter for the week, such a coincidence of Miss Bonneville seeking a seamstress and young Agnes displaying such skills would surely result in her getting the position, the next part of the plan and most difficult part was for Agnes to say where she was from, they had to come up with a solid story and not one that divulged she came from 1408, she could not tell any part of her unbelievable story and this Belle thought definitely the hardest part. Agnes looked more like something from a Shakespearian play. Belle though had been awake all night thinking, Agnes would have to present herself as being older she would have to adopt a foreign accent and declare herself a runaway orphan from Portugal, escaping the pending war and invasion from the French and Spanish. Agnes could say they had escaped Lisbon and travelled on a clutter class ship, she must say her parents had died whilst on board and that they were once tailors from Lisbon known for their intricate laces and fine tailoring. Jack was amazed by his Ma's incredible plot, quite how she had come up with it all he had no clue, he hugged her warmly and ran to work bursting to tell Avia later.

THE PAST OF BELLE

Belle was born into French aristocracy, the year was 1787 and by the time Belle was two years old the revolution had seized the country, it was a time of discontent and anger as the people starved, King Louis and his queen Marie Antoinette lived an opulent life style, spending obscene amounts of money in a senseless bourgeois way, they would both eventually without mercy face the guillotine. The revolution swept though France executing and exiling all of its aristocracy. Belle's family were smuggled out by a trusted servant in the depths of a cold dismal night, they were bundled aboard a ship leaving everything dear behind, they sailed to England where they were fortunate to have wealthy family connections, tragically after only three years of living in England Belle's parents both died of small pox, already suffering with poor health from their traumatic experiences and loss of a life style so decadent and glorious. Belle was left orphaned and alone, the house her parents had been kindly gifted was taken back by the Lord. He had little care for his French cousins and even less for their daughter and with no children of his own and no clue how to care for a child, he sent Belle away. She was sent to his cousin Lord Richard Colt Hoare at Stourton Hall, saying his home was unsuitable for the child. Belle would grow up under the care and management of the housekeeper Miss Bonneville and was trained from a young age to work in the house as a chamber maid, Lord Richard Hoare was never informed by his cousin of her aristocratic family background, had he have known Belle's life would have been very different. Belle was only young when Jeremiah Feld whisked her away to his farm. Belle would not have it any other way though she loved her husband and sons, her beginnings of finery never left Belle though, she was clever and elegant in her ways and her delicate features complimented her name Belle. Lord Richard Hoare being a man of great stature and wealth with his travelling and networking, one day heard of Belle's dreadful family tale through another French family who had suffered the same exile, he had never realised she was from aristocracy and was cross with his cousin for not informing him, he thought her just to be an illegitimate child sent away to be hidden from sight and suspicions, the poor girl had grown up in servants quarters in service to his Hall and now was married to a farmer with children, she could now never join higher society. Lord Richard Hoare after long consideration felt he needed to tell Belle, although he could not change the past he could shape her future and her sons for the better. One day he asked Belle for her company to walk with him around his gardens. Lord Richard Hoare told her of her family back ground, he was deeply sorry for his lack of interest in her case and was frustrated she had received such treatment, seeing Belle was content and had no wish now of mixing in the circles of aristocracy, Belle knew her husband Jeremiah was so proud and would never be able to accept he had a wife from French aristocracy, Jeremiah came from generations of farmers before him and she feared he would feel humiliated and unworthy. Lord Richard Hoare and Belle kept it their secret and sometimes he would invite her to walk with him around his magnificent gardens and she would tell her husband and sons how the lord liked to talk of his beloved lost wife, when in fact he mainly told her wonderful stories of his travels as if by enriching her mind, he freed her from her low position in society.

So Belle had easily found a story for Agnes the witch, for it was very like her own story and hers to give to another with hope. Belle met Agnes and Avia a week after the plan had been hatched, Avia was thrilled to meet Jack's Ma and Belle was very impressed with her bright and vivid character, she could now see why Jack talked about her so much, Belle felt nervous about meeting Agnes she was very superstitious about any kind of witch talk and still thought it was the devils work, her catholic routes were embedded in her soul, she also had a faint memory of something bad in her own past. Agnes though did not scare her, instead Belle like Avia felt an immediate bond, so much so she worried Agnes had woven a spell of enchantment upon them all, she was sweet and funny and all though her words were clumsy she had a grace more like a lost princess than a lost witch. Belle did not waste time and set about teaching her eager pupil, Agnes loved it and she learnt quicker than a fish in water. Belle would leave her with homework to do and the next time she visited Agnes, Agnes had elaborated her task, creating truly stunning work. Belle began to love her tutorials with the girls, even Miss Avia was trying to learn to sew, although she seemed happier with a trowel in her hand laughing with Jack. The little group set a date for the following Saturday, in the mean time Avia had to teach Agnes how to speak well with a slight foreign accent, to all their surprise Agnes already spoke a different language although no one was quite sure what it was, including Agnes who babbled away making them all giggle, their story was suddenly very convincing.

AVIA THE TEACHER

Agnes loved staying in the grand Hall with its elegant furniture and lavish decor, she stared in awe at the paintings of beautiful people adorned in the most wonderful attire each in stunning landscapes and she was fascinated with the collection of porcelain, clay and preserved animals, she was particularly amazed to see a Pangolin in the collection, she had strangely heard of such a creature. Avia said it was called taxidermy and Agnes seemed a little familiar with the process somewhere in her mind, Agnes especially loved all the rich fabrics and wonderful tapestries that told stories on the walls, she knew that to be found by Avia was the most amazing turn of fate. Avia taught her so well with such kindness and patience, Agnes was for ever in her debt and their bond was so deep nothing would ever stop Agnes from protecting her little saviour, Avia became a dedicated teacher and spent hours with Agnes educating her on things she thought any civilised young lady of the early 19th century should know, music lessons were the most difficult as Agnes had to be hidden completely or the plot was ruined. Avia had watched her household careful and had made notes with her poor writing of the times each member of the house did different chores and where they were in the house, her Father was away, he apparently was on a dig and not a dig like Avia's, he was with a whole team of archaeologists discovering interesting artefacts. Avia knew her sisters routine and discovered the maids did all the fires in the house at 6.30am ready to be lit for the waking household, Avia had a window of opportunity at 7am they had only fifteen minutes, Agnes was a special student though and had already learned enough of the piano to satisfy any one, should she be asked to play, Avia just had to build her repertoire a little more, her speech and writing were excelling and Agnes was helping Avia for some reason, by teaching Avia she learnt more herself and it was so much more interesting. Avia loved having Agnes staying in her room it was such fun, Agnes was amazing at hiding, when Lucy came into to do Avia's fire place, she was gone not a sense of her could be felt, seen or smelt. Sneaking Agnes in and out of the house was the hardest and most dangerous part always of their days, Avia though had dressed Agnes in Olivia's old clothes, they put her hair in a large bonnet and would sneak out of window and take cover in a large rhododendron bush, check the coast was clear and then dash to the ha-ha and stay low until under the cover of the woods, on wet days they were confined to creeping around the house and on these days cook would remark on Avia's endless appetite and laughed, she would turn into a horse or that she had hollow legs. Agnes had such an appetite for the Bath bun she found the brioche a delicacy, Avia told her the story of Solange Luyon a French Huguenot who escaped the French Protestants and fled to England, she arrived in Bath and peddled her buns on the streets from a basket, it was not long before her buns and beauty made her famous, she married a baker he stole her heart and her bun recipe. Agnes liked the story and would liked to have met her, Agnes asked Avia if she would like to become famous one day from her needlework, Avia and her fantasied they were amazingly and famous, Avia for her splendid gardens and Agnes her spectacular dress's. Strangely Avia thought to herself later as her little witch Agnes slept soundly on the other side of the bolster, that she would be famous she had a very special feeling about Agnes, herself though she knew fame was unlikely a lady was unlikely to be recognised for her gardening skills and she thought again of Solange Luyon and decided she must not be defeated, she would with Agnes's help invent the most wonderful flower. Avia drifted to sleep dreaming of beautiful dresses and gardens filled with exotic flowers, her dreams like always of late though turned to the fires and chants with strangers in bewitching dances.

TRUTH OR TALE

Belle loved her new girl friends, having spent most of her life surrounded by men, she was now experiencing the joy of chatter and giggling over silly nonsense, Avia had the most wonderful sense of humour and could see the funny side of everything, Agnes she found fascinating and although she was a witch, she was most definitely the kindest and most thoughtful one. Her sewing talent had surpassed any ones belief that she had picked up her first needle only a week ago, Belle insisted they must remain friends and an alliance grew strongly between the three unlikely companions, a little lady of gentry, a little witch of no fixed abode and a French farmers wife once of aristocracy. Belle though had a small thought that ran through her head each night she would lay awake and try to remember, it was a folk tale and something she saw as a young servant, something she had blocked from her memory. Slowly the thoughts and the tales and the memories came together, Belle suddenly knew why she felt little witch Agnes gave her that feeling of deja vu, feeling quite distressed Belle now remembered, she had arrived at Stourton Hall when she was six years old she was tall and strong despite her delicate features, Miss Bonnville was the new house keeper and she was young and kind and took the sad orphan under her wing, a little confused as to why she was with them. Belle would have to earn her keep and Miss Bonneville found her easy tasks around the house, she was delighted when she found Belle could speak French and the two although in a working relationship developed a fondness for each other, Belle would have to keep on her toes though, her house mistress was very insistent on perfection, punctuality, politeness and puritan ways. In return for good discipline and obedience she rewarded her household favourably and although she ran a tight ship it was a happy one with no grey areas. Belle did not mind any of this and enjoyed perfecting her work, she grew faster and more able and became at a very young age a competent house servant and was promoted to being the lady of the houses dresser, Belle adored the wonderful Beatrice Hoare and enjoyed looking after her, Beatrice was pleased and engaged with Belle's lovely tone and taste, being the ladies dresser gave Belle a good position in the house and she was respected by the other servants, her position also gave her far more freedom and she was able to take walks around the beautiful gardens and lake with lady Beatrice and alone, when alone Belle tended to be a little more adventurous and she would ramble off the paths and through the woodland, she loved this sense of freedom, one day there was a heavy frost so Lady Beatrice stayed warm by the fire afraid of a chill and a fall, Belle could not resist the beautiful bright afternoon though so once her chores were completed, she excused herself before the onslaught later of dressing duties for dinner. Belle found the woods less slippy and was enchanted by the frosty beauty that glistened amongst the leaves and cobwebs, she had probably gone a little too far, carried away with her exploring Belle became lost, she began to feel afraid and to panic Belle started to run, this only lead her deeper into the wood when she a glimpsed a little stone cottage and saw smoke, with no fear of the estate or it's occupants Belle went up to the curious little cottage, she knocked gently on the door she heard whispers and a rustle from within and slowly the door was opened a jar, Belle apologised for her intrusion and explained she was lost and asked if she could warm her feet and hands by the fire. The lady who answered the door was dressed in strange clothes in vivid colours with stunning embroidery, that seemed more appropriate for a summers day, she wore several beads and bangles and had strange markings painted on her hands and bare feet, her face was made up with some black around her eyes and red on her lips, Belle had never seen anyone so magnificent in her life and sat by the fire was another lady, so similar they had to have been sisters or twins, they offered Belle a drink that she gladly accepted and she was given a stool by the warm ambers of the fire, every so often they would add extra twigs which seemed to burn far more than a normal stick, her drink was sweet and thick and tasted heavily of cinnamon and camomile, Belle did not ask them many questions and excused herself feeling uncomfortable, they were very strange and spoke in such a funny way, she could hardly understand them, they both put on thick grey cloaks and offered to help her find the path, Belle did not argue, the night was bitterly cold and darkness began to fall, Belle confused just saw them disappear into thin air, she felt very strange and managed a few steps before falling Belle lay unable to move she tried to scream but nothing came out, luckily for Belle Jeremiah junior Feld was using the top path to see the bonfire for Hallows Eve at Stourton Hall, he lived at a farm on the estate and had come every year since he could remember, his parents had both died so at fourteen he was in charge of the farm and his two younger sisters. When he saw Belle lying there on the woody path, he did not hesitate to pick her up, Jeremiah was strong so her delicate frame was easy to carry and never did he walk so fast, he though she might die in his arms, Jeremiah got her back to the Hall and took her straight to the kitchens, he knew most of the servants of Stourton, with gasps she was well received and he was sent to find the search party with news she had been found. Belle was ill for several days she was kept warm in a room with a fire and they had the Doctor visit her, he said it was as though she had been poisoned, he did not know if she would survive, she tossed and turned and cried out in her dreams. Then one Saturday Belle woke feeling fine, although very confused she remembered nothing and never did until she saw Agnes. Jeremiah remembered everything of that night and he called to see Belle whenever he could, that night what ever happened Belle felt was magical, for Jeremiah who had found her was the kindest and loveliest man on God's earth to her. Belle and Jeremiah courted for a few years, he charmed her in any way he knew and gave her gifts, mainly for Belle though he made her laugh and they chatted for hours, he was the best friend she had ever had and on her sixteenth birthday he proposed. Belle missed the finery of Stourton Hall and her ladyship and Miss Bonevilllle, she was happy though to have a good husband who she loved and a pretty stone farm house with roses around the door. The revelation for Belle to remember that night of her past was enormous to her. The villagers and Hall staff and family had questioned for years what happened to Belle that night, many told the stories they had grown up with about the witches in Stourton woods, young girls had gone missing from time to time and some like Belle had been found in a state of delirium and always on All Hallows Eve, there were lots of different folk tales, Belle suddenly realised though they were all true her mind reeled, she was only certain of one thing her fear of the dark and woods since that night was for good reason, Belle had met the witches and had been in their lair. She also knew if it wasn't for Jeremiah finding her that cold night she would never had survived and she thought back to the witches and how they held her as they walked her in the woods, Belle had a strange feeling they were taking her not guiding her home. She remembered they talked about something they had lost, they looked for something Belle felt dizzy did they look for Agnes all those years ago.

ONE LITTLE WITCH
GOES TO MARKET

It was a fine day and Avia and Agnes crept out of the house after doing their final preparations, only this time Agnes wore her favourite blue dress she had altered it perfectly, Avia had set her hair in ringlets and her thick black shiny hair cascaded around her perfect little face, she wore jewellery that they had found in the cavern underground; Jack had created a dig and excavated many treasures, Avia and Agnes would log each one and they would hide them in the cottage attic. Agnes wore Olivia's old cloak and carried a basket with gloves and petticoats she and Belle had made, each with exquisite embroidery. As planned they met Jack at the Gothic cottage on the morning of market day, Jack was there waiting for them as promised, Avia lit up like star when she saw his smiling face and although nervous they chatted as normal. Jack and Avia had shown Agnes the way to the market a few days before, she had plenty of time that morning and would be safe as lots of villagers and traders would be on the track. Agnes was terribly nervous though that something could go wrong, Avia assured her she would be fine, she just had to be confident and remember her story and not say to much, they walked with her part way through the woods and got her to the track that lead to the market, Avia suddenly felt terribly anxious herself as she wished her friend luck and waved her off, what if something did go dreadfully wrong, Agnes waved and disappeared around the bend, Jack reassured Avia on the way back to the cottage Agnes would be fine after all she was a witch. Avia and Jack to keep their minds busy worked on the cottage garden, Avia had designed a wrought iron gazebo with the blacksmith, the beautifully made structure now stood proudly in the garden with its intricate metal flower work, they planted roses at each corner and then planted buxom in diagonals, Avia wanted to create a tudor knot garden, as they worked Jack and Avia chatted about there dreams and hopes both laughed as they both wanted the same thing to be famous garden designers. Avia enjoyed just being with Jack again, she was so terribly found of Agnes, lately though she had taken all her time and she hadn't been to see her friend Lottie for weeks, partly because she was afraid she would let something slip and Lottie as lovely as she was, could most definitely not be trusted. Avia dearly hoped that their plan was working and Miss Bonneville and Agnes had met. A hundred different scenarios went through Avia's mind sending her into an oblivion of panic. As though Jack read her mind he took Avia's hand and lead her away from the cottage, they walked towards the Temple of Apollo. Together they ran hand in hand up the steep steps and stood looking over the beautiful gardens and lake and prayed out loud for their plot to work. Avia wanted that moment to last forever standing there with Jack holding his hand and looking at the beautiful view, she thought he felt the same because he just stood there with her, the church bell struck twelve breaking their trances, both agreed they should go for lunch then meet back at the cottage and wait for Agnes still holding hands they ran down the cobbled path then parted company. Avia ran back to the hall her cheeks glowed from the bright sunshine and fresh air, she felt so happy to have Jack as her friend and Avia wished they could be together forever. Lunch was difficult as her sisters asked her to many questions, intrigued as to what their sister was up to all the time, she explained about her garden and then spent the whole hour persuading them to visit it another day as she wanted them to see it when the fountain and pond had been finished, they reluctantly agreed and then suggested they should call for the carriage and visit Thomas and his sister Edwina, Avia then had to worm her way out of the social visit, saying she had arranged to work with Jack, they were very persistent but agreed they would go without her, with relief Avia escaped bidding them a pleasant stay with Thomas and sent her regards to Edwina, apparently Thomas had guests and Avia had the feeling it was more a plan to meet them, they were friends from Petworth in Sussex, Cecilia no doubt hoped to meet George Wyndham his Father was a collector of wonderful art and they were very wealthy. Avia ran down the path towards the cottage she didn't wish for all the wealth and place in society as her sisters did, Avia fancied a simpler life and one in which she was free to garden. Jack was waiting and grinned his lovely grin, they both sat on the stone bench below the gothic window and waited, if all had gone well Agnes would have met Miss Bonneville at Belle's cheese stall. Their wait was long they were happy though and just sat together spotting different birds and naming all they saw. They listened to bird song, Jack as always was good at imitating them, to keep themselves warm they started climbing the yew tree, Jack help Avia and they sat on one of the big branches, as they looked up they saw hanging in the branches lots of metal charms all with different symbols, they were old and rusty, Avia felt a shudder as though they were being watched although this time it felt different from Agnes, this felt scary. Jack sensed the feeling to and they both got down, they needed to ask Agnes if she knew anything about the charms and symbols, there was still no sign of Agnes though, so they started to walk up to the track to meet her, Avia started to worry as the afternoon light started to fade, Agnes was really late now and she like Jack would have to get back home. They waited as long as they could, the woods started to grow dark quickly and still they felt watched, Jack was sure he had seen and heard something, he glanced back to see a swish of colours disappear into the trees, someone or thing was definitely watching them, Jack worried for Avia's safety and walked her back to the Hall, he saw her go in the door to the kitchens and left for the farm. When he got back his Mother was back from market, she had had a good day, they were all happily chatting and laughing, Jack was so pleased to see them he felt blessed with his family and went to help clear out the cart, as he listened to his Ma gabble on excitedly about the days events, she told the tale of the peddler girl with fancy gloves who came to her stall and met Miss Bonneville from the Hall, Belle then explained how she employed her there and then for the position of a seamstress, she told Jeremiah about the stunning embroidery and the girl with the darkest hair and beautiful dress, Jeremiah listened and then said to Belle she must choose some fabric, he would take her to town and this new seamstress could make her a fancy dress to wear on market day, Belle smiled with glee and said she would love that more than anything, Jack then dared to ask casually where this peddler girl came from and Belle just replied she wasn't sure but it was not from these parts, she said he would probably meet her as she was taken by Miss Bonneville straight to Stourton Hall, Jack smiled at his Ma and muttered thank the lord, Avia would know soon to he hoped, although in that massive Hall it was possible she would not. Jack was happy though the plan had worked and Belle seemed very pleased, Jack was worried though something was strange about those symbols in the tree and something didn't feel good, both Avia and himself had felt scared by their watcher in the woods, Jack had seen someone a few times now in the trees, he only got small glimpses though of ruffling dress's and cloaks and he had felt uneasy for a while, he didn't want to scare Miss Avia to much though, although he feared something strange was a foot, he hoped her and Miss Avia hadn't let the devil in the door with their plots and deception.

THE SEAMSTRESS OF STOURTON

Agnes felt so nervous as she walked into the town she could feel the towns folk and traders stare at her unusual looks and dress, she held her head up high and walked proudly with a smile on her face, just like Miss Avia had taught her in the library with books on her head, she looked at the stalls and showed her work and then went over to Belle's cheese stall, Belle gave her some cheese as planned and Agnes spent ages choosing a piece, then when Miss Bonneville appeared, as instructed by Avia, Agnes started to show Belle her needlework and say how she sought work and somewhere to live, Agnes could not believe how well it went Miss Bonneville instantly loved her work and was impressed with Agnes's knowledge and skills. Belle and Miss Bonneville chatted about old times, while Agnes stood there taking everything in, she stared around the market and an old memory stirred of her stood by her mother at a stall with clay pots full of potions, there were other stalls all around and fires, straw was on the floor and folk were mainly dressed in thick furs, it was bitterly cold flurries of snow swirled in the air deciding not to settle they went else where, then Agnes remembered them packing up and going early, she remembered getting ready for Samhain and her mother with her friends by the fire and then nothing, Agnes started to feel a little panicky and angry inside, what had they done to her and why did they hide her and why didn't they come back for her, it was four hundred years ago, then Agnes heard Belle's sweet voice, she spoke to Miss Bonneville saying the poor girl must be half starved and with that it was agreed, Miss Bonneville asked Agnes if she was able to get her belongings another day she should come to the Hall straight away. Agnes got into the carriage with Miss Bonneville and they wrapped blankets around themselves, forgetting her anger and panic Agnes began to enjoy the carriage ride and excitement that she had done it. Avia and Jack would be so proud of her and how wonderful, she would have a room and food and she was a seamstress, Agnes decided that day she would concentrate on creating the most wonderful needle work, maybe the odd little spell of magic could be sewn or seeded for Avia her most special friend, Agnes also thought to herself as they trundled along if there was ever a need she would protect her new friends in anyway she could, as the pretty woods and fields fluttered by Agnes felt a sense that something bad was on it's way and she had to be strong and ready, in the walls of Stourton Hall she hoped she was safe, the cottage though that was a place where trouble could come, as soon as she was able she must find a way to put up a guarding spell to keep evil spirits or witches out, Agnes thought back to the memory of her mother the market and Samhain, what ever had happened and why Agnes was not sure, the only thing she did fear was that her mother and friends would come back for her, Agnes wanted to stay here with Avia and Jack she felt safe a feeling she had never felt before, with her mother there was always fear and persecution from others. Agnes began to suspect, her mother the witch and her coven were not perhaps as good as she had thought.

Agnes felt very grand as they arrived at Stourton Hall even the servants entrance felt wonderful, the lower floor halls lead to the kitchen, scullery, boot room and so much more, it felt warm and smelt delicious she was taken to the huge kitchen and sat at the large wooden scrubbed table, the cook eyed her up and down and called her a fancy piece with a twinkle in her eye, she instructed the maid Bonnie to give her a large bowl of stew and a huge hunk of bread she was also given a tankard of ale, Agnes did not like the bitter taste and unafraid asked Bonnie if she could try another drink, Bonnie happily drank the ale and got Agnes some Barley water from the pantry, Bonnie sat down and some other servants arrived and ate stew and bread, they chatted about the day as others appeared and disappeared ate and cleared, Agnes was given a piece of apple pie with thick sweet cream, she then copied the other servants clearing her plates and asked what she was to do, Miss Bonneville arrived instantly and took Agnes to the servants bedroom quarters, Agnes had a room high in the eaves she had a pretty window that looked over the tree tops, there was a neat single bed, chair and a large dresser with a mirror and wash basin, a little fire crackled away with extra logs by the side, on the bed folded neatly was a towel and uniform with a sturdy pair of shoes, on the pillow a starched bed gown was folded with a knitted shawl, Agnes pinched herself to check this was all real, Miss Bonneville smiled seeing her delight and instructed her to change, then meet her in her office opposite the kitchen, they could then discuss her wages and work schedule, Agnes waited until she had heard Miss Bonneville go down the stairs then she gave a squeal of excitement, she had heard Jack talk of wages with Avia, he said Stourton Hall paid their servant the best wages, Agnes had not thought she would be paid to have a room, a roof and a fire was more than a dream and food they were going to give her food, Agnes knew she was the luckiest girl a live and nothing on the earth would make her want to leave, she quickly dressed into her uniform and pinned her hair up neatly, Agnes looked at herself in the mirror wiped her face and admired her crisp pale blue dress and piny all lined with delicate lace, she noticed the others wore a black dress with a white piny and the men a black suit and crisp white shirt. Agnes quickly made her way to the office glancing back at her room, so she did not forget the way, Agnes found the office, she knocked and went in and took a seat opposite Miss Bonneville, the office was neat as a pin with shelves of books on all sorts of things, Miss Bonneville opened a file and started to write as she wrote she explained that Agnes would earn two pence a week and was aloud to take other work in her own time, she would work from seven until three and then be on call from six until eight for any fixing issues amongst the household. Her main work was completing a new wardrobe for Miss Cecilia and then Miss

Olivia, they would go to Bath next week and choose fabrics, Miss Bonneville then asked her to follow, they walked up the stairs into the main house. Agnes already knew the house it felt strange to pretend she had never set eyes on its beauty before, she also knew they were heading for Avia's wing, Agnes felt a flush of nerves as they walked into the gracious sitting area, Avia was starring out of the window and turned trying hard to hide her instant surprise and pleasure to see her dear little witch, Olivia was concentrating on her embroidery and slowly looked up to see the curious new comer she faintly smiled, Cecilia immediately put down her book and walked over to great Agnes, when the girls realised she was to be the seamstress and make all their new dresses they giggled with excitement and chatter and on learning they were to visit Bath to buy some fashionable fabrics they bubbled over, even Avia showed an interest in having a new frock. Agnes was shown their dress collection and given a few that needed repair and a few that needed throwing, on leaving the girls she asked Miss Bonneville if she may make herself something from the discarded dress's to wear to Bath, she agreed, Agnes sensed Miss Bonneville now knew she had no other processions other than the ones on her back, Agnes was then lead back over to the servants quarters, they went up a little set of stairs that lead to one large room with the most amazing half sloped glass roof and windows that reach the ceiling and floor, there was a large table and shelves with every sewing thing imaginable in labeled boxes, there was a grand fireplace on the back wall that had just been lit, on its large mantle was a stone statue of a wild cat in a glass box, that starred endlessly towards the door as if forever on guard, Miss Bonneville then said her breakfast was served in the kitchen at eight her lunch at twelve and supper at six, Miss Bonneville said any question she must ask her and not other members of staff and she was not to gossip or talk about others behind their backs, then she went through a list of rules and finally finished by saying she could start work on Monday, this gave Agnes a whole day off and plenty of time to re-pair and redesign her discarded dresses. Miss Bonneville left her and Agnes set about hanging the dresses and finding all the things she needed to sew. Agnes looked at the wild cat on the mantle when she was a witches daughter in the woods, she used to play with one just the same, she had called her Hestia as her Mother said they once had a cat with that name. Agnes couldn't help herself and carefully took the stone wild cat out of the glass box and just breathed a little life back to her, soon Hestia was purring around her and sat dutifully next to her cleaning her paws as though she had always sat there. Agnes knew it was wrong to already do magic, Hestia would be useful though and it was good to have little companion every good witch needed some sort of pet. Elated she started work and sewed by candle light as the light had left the day far behind, once the fire had died to embers, she left with her candle and went to the kitchen, cook showed her how to make a tea and gave her some biscuits she sat at the table joined by Bonnie, Martha and Lucy who seemed thrilled to meet her, Agnes had to be careful though and was very vague when asked questions about her past, keeping strictly to her story word for word. Agnes exhausted excused herself pouring a mug of milk she went to her bedroom, Hestia was curled up by the fire, Agnes gave her the mug of milk and chatted to her about the day, sleepily Agnes drifted of to sleep in her cosy room in wonder at her new life at the wonderful Stourton Hall.

THE PAST OF AVOCA 1208

Avoca didn't remember much of her childhood, other than always being hungry and travelling across deserts, each city or village they would pass through and stay only for however long it took to replenish supplies, selling spices and charms. They travelled in a large caravans of people, safety in numbers was their only reason, for they fought and spatted amongst each other for food and supplies, survival was hard Avoca remembered looking at her mother and wondered how her frail body and furrowed face survived the rat race, she was kind to her children and fed them what she could, Avoca knew she stole to give them things, her hands were like lighting and she seemed to disappear once the deed was done so frail and bent no one could imagine her a threat. Avoca's father though was strong and loud he used force for any crime and would kill with his bare hands when times were hard. Avoca remembered the day her mother passed away vividly, she remembered setting her out in the burning boat on the river, the smell of smoke lingered in her memory for years and even now a bonfire could stir emotion deep in her soul, where now only revenge lay deep inside. Not long after Avoca's mother's death they would arrive in a city with great white walls a fortress that spread for miles, it wound its way down to a huge river where elephants and locals bathed, boats larger than Avoca had ever seen before roared like monsters in the huge rivers mouth, waiting for the little boats to load sacks of produce. Avoca was amazed by the huge citadel with its smells and people, crowds of so many different types gathered, sounds and singing Avoca had never heard rang with bells as they toiled across the city skies, calling out chants and prayers with words Avoca did not understand. When night fall came they settled by the river with other travellers and each spoke to one another relaying news of other lands and opportunity, sadly for Avoca and her sisters this bought news to their father of payment in gold for good child stock and by the next evening Avoca and her sisters were taken from the wooden caravan their home and placed in a cold stone chamber beneath the ground, Avoca could see bars and no escape, her sisters cried for their father he never came, Avoca knew he had sold them she saw the exchange of money, if only she had known the terms. Several days later with their eyes squinting from the sun, Avoca and her sisters and other girls were bought to a pen they were ringed by the ankles attached to a rock and inspected by their prospective owners, they looked at their teeth and pulled on their hair, each child was taken, Avoca saw her sisters go they were bought by the same lady and man she prayed they were not cruel and would not work them to hard, Avoca was left to the very last and stood alone in the searing sun with no shade, she did not no why she had good teeth and hair, she began to feel even more scared, then a woman arrived wrapped in silks and laden with jewels, she had her ring and rock removed and bid Agnes follow her, they got into a trap pulled by a donkey and were lead through the maze of walls, eventually they arrived at the huge palace that sat on the top of the citadel, Agnes with no word was ushered along into a chamber where lots of other girls chatted and busied themselves and with no word Avoca was left with the girls, before long a girl who looked just like her approached Avoca and lead her to a bathing area, she was then dressed in beautiful silks and had her face, hand and feet painted with henna, she then sat with the others in a large court yard and older women bought them food on platters, she watched the others as they helped themselves filling their clay bowls, Avoca ate well and then listened to the others talk she began to understand their words much like her own with a slight difference, the girl next to her told Agnes her name was Josina and she seemed very curious about Avoca and stayed by her side, she was helpful teaching her how things worked in the palace, when Agnes asked what they were all doing there, she laughed and said when she was older she would be taken to the Prince to be his wife with lots of others, Avoca was shocked, Josina calmed her though and said quietly not to worry by then they would be long gone. The palace chambers were comfortable and Avoca enjoyed the gorgeous food, she loved swimming in the warm waters and wandering in grounds with scented trees and flowers, Josina had started to teach her many things one was writing on slates with stone she taught her how each mark made up her words and showed how she recorded her recipes on cloth she painted with dye. Avoca was not unhappy with her situation although she was a prisoner and property of the palace, in time she yearned to be free and travel, Josina sensed her restlessness and asked her to be patient, she said it would not be long and she explained something to Avoca she did not fully understand, Josina told her she was born under a moon that gave her special gifts that meant like Josina she could travel between times and places, this though could only happen on the night of Samhain. When Avoca asked why she stayed prisoner in the palace Josina admitted she had been tricked, although she said it was beneficial to her, Josina said she travelled to the past of places and times learning others knowledge, the palace it seemed had a wealth of scholars in apothecary, she had also learnt some wonderful conjuring. Josina said though they would leave the next night, although excited Avoca was nervous these walls had offered her protection and good health, although she knew escape was her only route, Avoca did not wish to be a wife ever. The Eve of Samhain as Josina named it arrived quickly and as the chimes were heard across the city calling for evening prayers, Josina and Avoca stood with their silk bags full of as much as they could carry, they were dressed in so much they were stifled by the heat of the evening even though the temperature had dropped, Josina lit a small fire hidden in the grounds she spoke her rhyme in her magical voice, as soon as the moon was alined they disappeared, they left only ambers of dust. The guards of the palace who searched for the missing prisoners later believed they had vanished into the flames to die, so no search or questions were asked, they were just two slave girls who's strange disappearance was of no consequence to anyone. Avoca and Josina crashed onto the streets of London. The air was thick with smoke and the cold was like nothing Avoca had felt before, Josina quickly found them lodgings above a noisy tavern, men whistled and called at them as they passed, Josina rustled Avoca along, they entered the dark room with a large fire that glowed in the open stone hearth it had a small set of stairs that lead to a bed, Josina opened the curtains that let in the lights of the fires and the smell of smoke, Josina said they would take it and paid the grumpy hag some coins, she told Avoca the year was 1400 and she would not stay long, they ate a bowl of pottage and slept in the lumpy bed. Avoka and Josina the next morning travelled by foot through the filthy streets to Fenchurch, here they visited an Alchemists shop, it smelt very strange and had deep shelves containing pots of different potions and stuffed animals, a middle aged gentleman neatly dressed with an over piny greeted them cautiously noting their strange attire, Josina spoke in webs to him and wound her story around him like a spider would spin her silk thread. With no word from Josina and no clue what was happening Avoca was left with the dumb founded Alchemist, he showed Avoca to the back of the shop where he made his potions and pastes, Avoca watched she was then shown where to get water from and how to boil it, he seemed of pleasant nature and was patient realising his new assistant spoke no English, Avoca though was a very fast learner and she was obedient, Dastin began to enjoy the company of his strange new apprentice as she learnt quickly he relied more and more on her skills and he shared more knowledge with her, Dastin let her look at his books and slowly Avoca realised Josina's plan, Eliphas Dastin was a warlock who worked under the cover as an alchemist, he proudly boasted to Avoca of his history of generations of notorious warlocks before him and he knew secrets and mixes not even recorded in his fathers works, he warned Avoca of his brother who was younger and did not remember his Father he had been taken as a soldier for the King. Avoca understood this was a warning to keep quiet. Eliphas looked after her he would often give her potions to help her sleep, most she would throw some though he would watch her drink and she would sleep with strange dreams. Most evenings Avoca would excuse herself and record her findings at night in her little room above the shop, she had fabric scraps from sack and dye from a paste she made. Josina would be pleased and Avoca felt happier she knew of her plan, the next year came and so did Josina on the blast of a bitterly cold wind, Avoca was ready to leave her little bag packed and with no word to Dastin she intended to leave and not return. Josina was stood outside in the little courtyard her fire all ready lit, the girls greeted each other with joy; then Josina looked at Avoca with dread, for one thing that Avoca had not known or planned was that she would carry a child, Avoca had no clue and cried she had been tricked by potions and now did not know what to do, Josina tried her best to comfort her but explained the travel would kill her she had no choice but to go back to Dastin. Josina promised she would be back and Josina left on that bitter night, poor Avoca crept back to her tiny bed and she smouldered away as she wept, Dastin would pay after the child was born, for his trickery, she kept to her word and worked away she stole and sneaked from her master. When Dastin knew of the child he seemed not unpleased and in a strange little church up on a hill, Eliphas Dastin married his apprentice as not to shame himself or her. The baby was born and Josina still did not appear the following year, Avoca tried as hard as she could to live the lie with her husband Dastin by her side, the infant was sweet and Agnes was her chosen name, still Josina did not come and Avoca could take no more, Dastin had grown colder and cruel in his ways and one night she would break and with a trick Josina had shown her she would take his life away. Avoca left with all that she could carry in a cart with her little Agnes on the top, she pushed the cart through the streets and headed for the countryside where she could hide. Dastin as warned left her a trail of trouble for he had a sherif as a brother, once a soldier he was now a powerful man, knowing his brother had taken a wife and had a child, the brother search for her, he sought permission from the King to find the murderer and have her hung, he was in great favour with the King Henry IV after the defeat of traitors, who had grown a rebel army to kill the King, instead the traitors heads would fall including the leader of the conspiracy Harry Hotspur. Tobias Dastin was granted permission by the King to take three men and horses and search the land, he would bring the wife to trial, for foul play in the matter of the strange death of his brother Eliphas Dastin, with no mark on him he was found literally, a dead man standing, there was also a matter of theft to deal with all his money was gone. Avoca knew she would be hunted so she kept to the forest for over a year travelling slowly with Agnes, she wanted to leave each night of Samhain all Hallows Eve, she never had the knowledge or the heart to leave her little Agnes though, with her sweet and precious little ways. Avoca struggled on until one sweet day she found a pretty track by a stream and as she headed up the hill, Avoca looked over a valley of such beauty and charm she knew she was at home.

YARDS OF LACE
& FIREWORKS

Avia woke up very early it was Monday morning she was so excited today she would go to Bath with her sisters and Agnes, she could not believe how well their plan had worked and she had nearly screamed for joy when she saw Agnes with Miss Bonneville, she had been so stressed that Agnes was lost forever on market day, to see her turn up in their sitting room was a pleasure beyond belief, Avia had spent Sunday in the garden with Jack and left Agnes to settle in, they also needed to be double careful they caused no suspicion, Avia packed a special celebratory picnic with Bonnie's help saying it was to thank Jack for all his hard work, Bonnie being sweet would not breathe a word and said how wonderful Jack was, Avia unsure if she liked how much Bonnie went on about how wonderful Jack was, thanked her gracefully and left with the picnic, Jack was thrilled and they sat admiring their work by the new water feature with a large urn fountain, Avia thanked Jack so much for his help, Jack expressed his concern though to Avia after they had giggled and chatted, he took on a serious note and told her of some of the old tales of witches in Stourton woods, he begged Avia to be careful at the cottage and asked her not to go alone. Avia at first was defensive proclaiming she was fine and could look after herself, Jack grew a little cross though, so she decided to obey his wishes, Jack thanked her and promised her he would visit the cottage as often as possible and help so she would never be alone in the garden. Jack then told her Belle's story and how for the first time in years and since seeing Agnes, she had remembered that night and the witches and the cottage. Belle had asked Jack to tell Avia in confidence as she was genuinely worried for her safety, she believed the witches came back. Avia was very shocked by his story although believed Belle completely, they both wondered if they would come back again and if it was Agnes they looked for, Avia said they would talk to Agnes, she was surely in grave danger, if they came back for her, maybe they had taken other young girls instead of Agnes over the centuries. Avia shuddered with fear and thought Jack was right it was no longer safe by the cottage alone, as if to confirm this they heard a rustle and a small screeched from behind the cottage, Jack quickly got up and ran just in time to see the ruffle of dress's disappear and that strange smell lingered of pungent herbs and smoke, he came back to Avia saying they definitely had company, normally they would send for Otto and Benny only they feared that would be no help against a witch in the woods. Jack walked Avia back up to the house and he wished her a pleasant trip to Bath, he teased her for having fancy frocks made for her, Avia didn't mind for some reason everything jack said these days made her laugh, or she found herself listening to him with the greatest respect, she waved him off, as always regretting they would not see each other for a few days. The next morning arrived quickly and Avia lay in bed as she heard her sisters giggle with excitement, whilst calling her to hurry up and dress for breakfast. The carriage waited for them with the horses impatiently stamping their hooves, Avia went straight to the horses and patted them giving them each a sugar lump from the breakfast table, Miss Bonneville and the girls put their travel blankets across them and soon they were off, with the wheels crunching on the gravel. Avia starred out as they left, she didn't like to leave and then she saw Jack by the walled garden waving with his infectious grin, Avia waved back and heard sighs from her sisters and little scolds for being so friendly with a grounds boy, Avia did not react and shared a little grin with Agnes who sat quietly next to Miss Bonneville. The journey was slow until they reached the turnpike to Bath, they arrived exhausted from being juddered around. Their lodgings were at Sydney Place, they stayed with their Great Aunt Eliza who had been widowed for many years, she still wore black and mainly stayed in her room, the house was not as lavish as the girls were used to, they happily though made themselves at home, engaging with their host, Cecilia was Aunt Eliza's favourite as she was the first born, she twinkled with joy when she saw her and was a happy to see the other sisters only a little less enamoured, Avia was not put out like Olivia, she gladly accepted the gifted pound each niece was given to spend in Bath, her Aunt said she had no use of her late husbands stash. Avia had already decided she would save hers for seeds and bulbs and with hope buy a book. After a strange lunch of peas pudding, the girls excitedly set off a long Great Pulteney, enjoying the crisp sunny afternoon, the streets of Bath were bustling with fashionable ladies from London, Cecilia and Olivia studied them in detail considering this an important research for their new wardrobe, whilst Avia walked with her head in the clouds admiring the architecture. They arrived on Milson Street and were directed by Miss Bonneville straight to the drapers and haberdashery store, even Avia was amazed by the amount of choice, she wonder how an earth they would choose from all the fabrics, buttons and lace, as soon as they walked in a little team of ladies in uniforms started helping the Stourton girls, this made their task so much easier, they showed them paintings of fashions and showed them the latest colours and complimenting accessories and styles the process had begun, Agnes was engrossed in the paintings and she consumed every detail to the last stitch, she felt so important and hardly had chance to even look at her friend Avia, Avia understood her work though and escaped asking directions for the book store, it was just a couple of doors down as she entered the bell rang and an old gentlemen in pinstripes with glass's came forward to assist her, she explained her interest in garden design and said she would like the latest book. The gentleman scuffled off to the back of the musty shop, saying very little, a little later he bought back in his clutches a large red book and with gloves on, he put it on the table for Avia to look at, he gestured she put the cotton gloves on over her gloves, the book was illustrated like her others by Repton, only this one gave a more modern approach, the book reached a larger audience and not just the elite, it was perfect; Avia enquired for the price, noting to the book seller it had a scratch on its jacket, he tutted and went away again returning with a price written neatly in ink, the price was ten shillings this was half of her pound, Avia knew some people didn't earn that in a year, the pound was gift though and she still would have money for seeds and bulbs most of which she could get for free, she cared not for buying anything else and her conscience as if a completely different person agreed, she thought of Jack and how he would love to look at the book , so it was decided the book seller a little surprised by her interest and wealth accepted her pound, he wrote down her address and came back with her change, a younger man came to the front of the shop and bid her farewell with thanks, he then added that if she should change her mind she could bring it back, Avia thanked him and assured him she would not, he then boldly asked if she would like to watch the fireworks in Sydney park in the evening, he had free tickets she explained they were a rather large party of five ladies, he happily gave her five tickets and said he looked forward to seeing her there and gave her a receipt for the book, saying it would be delivered later that day to her town address, she thanked him immensely and hurried back to the drapers. Avia had to quickly decide upon her fabric, pretending she had been engrossed by the buttons, for Avia it was easy Agnes had noticed her absence and covered for her friend, choosing her the most beautiful embroiled pale blue and white fabric, with complimentary white lace and little blue buttons; as Avia would not be whirled out on the busy social calendar like her eldest sister, one dress was enough, Avia was thrilled with Agnes's choice she adored the painting of the pattern Agnes was going to make it into. Miss Bonneville was very impressed with Agnes and marvelled at how she helped with the fabric choosing and matching of things so delicately, her girls would be the best dressed of the season, Miss Bonneville felt a flush of pride and felt luck was on her side. They all then descended upon the Pump Rooms and had afternoon tea, the room bustled with mainly young ladies accompanied by their Mothers and other chaperones, Avia unlike her sisters who people watched intently looked with interest at the wonderful paintings by Hoare and Gainsborough, she loved all the portraits she had seen by Gainsborough, his paintings made everyone looked so beautiful and the landscapes were exquisite. Cecilia and Olivia ignored their little sisters comments distracted by a group that had just entered the room, Thomas and his sister Edwina were among the fashionable group, Edwina came straight over seeing Olivia and bubbled over with excitement, her calmer brother also came over clearly delighted to see Olivia, they all chatted and then Thomas said about the music and fireworks in Sydney Gardens later, Olivia sighed disappointment not sure Miss Bonneville would permit it, when Avia to everyones surprise pulled five tickets out of her skirt pockets, declaring I think she will if we can all go and its is only over the path, everyone laughed in amazement at Avia not one of them thought to ask how she got them, as if on cue, Miss Bonneville returned from her chores and happily agreed they could all go as long as they stayed close to one another, to have Thomas in the party would be even more appropriate. So it was settled and they all met at the entrance that evening dressed in their Saturday best. Never had Avia seen anything so wonderful and this was her chance to walk arm in arm with Agnes as Miss Bonneville approved each had a partner and Olivia was more than safe with both Thomas and Edwina at her side, the park was full of well dressed people who seemed quite well acquainted, music played form a band stand and little stalls sold hot chestnuts, pies and other delicacies, drinks were sold at long trestle tables, pretty lanterns in colours and bunting decorated the trees and candle lamps, exploring the well lit park with all its oddities it was very entertaining and at times a little scary, Avia felt she was in some exotic country far away with all the colours and smells. When it was late the firework display was set off and the pretty lights lit up the skies, Agnes stared in disbelief and Avia clutched her friend quite terrified by the noises, she wished Jack was here to see all this and could not wait to tell him, as they walked back Agnes had chance to talk as the others hung back in their chatter, Agnes babbled about how happy she was and how wonderful it was to able to work and live in the Hall, Avia squeezed her hand and just listened with joy, tonight she would not ruin her pleasure by scaring her with Jacks story of Belle's encounter with the witches, they would have to do that another day. As they walked towards the gates she saw the book shop man and thanked him graciously for the tickets, he happily accepted and bustled off with a pretty lady on his arm, behind him a strange lady with a bent over back wrapped in cloaks approached them, she held a basket with wheat charms all intricately woven into different shapes of hearts, animals or people, she began her patter to Avia and Agnes and tried to peddle them some charms from her basket, saying they were lucky and would bring them fortune and love, Avia thought she already had a fortune so was a little dismissive, the old lady looked up from under her cloak, then shrank away like a whimpering animal as if in pain, mumbling something about curses and promises, she looked at Agnes and bowed deeply offering them both a wheat owl for free. Agnes felt some strange tension between her and the old woman straight away she could not explain, she heard words in her head and felt the urge to raise her arms towards the old lady, she managed though to not speak or act, her eyes conveyed her message somehow to the old hag to be well gone from her and Miss Avia. Miss Bonneville and the others rushed over, the old lady in cloaks by now had scuttled off into the darkness, Agnes looked shaken as did Avia, Avia knew something was strange and her little witch had something going on that she battled from within, trying hard to play down the whole event, she proclaimed that the poor old lady was not of sound mind and she feared she had been drinking to much Gin, assured everyone was fine, the party moved on although Avia noticed that now Miss Bonneville walked with her and Agnes probably to check they were fine and also because Cecilia walked with a tall gentleman named George from Petworth, Avia broke the ice and giggled to her walking companions that all those beautiful dress's may be of no need after all, she thought her sisters had already found their suiters, Miss Bonneville tutted at her, although she would no doubt have to agree, the two older Stourton girls were already it seemed in the company of two very honourable well born friends. Exhausted the party bid their farewells and retired for the evening, Agnes managed to talk quietly to Avia about the old hag, she felt nervous about the situation and said she did not understand why she felt the need to be cruel to the poor old thing, Avia had already conspired her own theory, she thought a little like society, witches also had a hierarchy and she thought Agnes was right at the top just like royalty, Avia made her giggle by saying she was a Princess of witches. Agnes accepted her prognosis with thought and gratitude and seemed more settled. The next morning was bright and Avia could not wait to leave the bustle of Bath and longed to be back in the gardens and peaceful fresh air, her sisters however had managed to persuade Miss Bonneville that they could stay and socialise, under their Aunts guidance, with strict rules and instructions they were left behind and a much more roomy carriage ride was taken back to the Hall, Avia was worried though her little witch looked drained and perplexed, she had to some how talk to her with Jack, it would be impossible though for the rest of the week, she would be so busy sewing endless hems and tucks. The small party home all seemed lost in their own thoughts and the arrival back to Stourton Hall was swift. Agnes whispered as she got out from the carriage for Avia to meet her that afternoon before dark at the cottage. Somehow Avia had to find Jack and quickly she made her excuses and ran.

FAILING & FALLING

Life had become very hard for Josina and Avoca after the battle and seizure of the Fort, the death of their beloved queen hurt them more than they could bare, they mourned her loss and their own loss, hardship had fallen on many, they lived in a cave deep in the mountain hidden by the forest and lived of what they hunted and foraged for, times had become violent so they had to protect themselves, they waited impatiently for the next Samhain and planned to go back to Stourton Castle. Josina was thrown by the years and moons though her precious book of time was lost in their escape, so their visit would be a random year, Josina could remember enough though to hopefully land them were Agnes was buried in the cavern and after the witch hunt for Avoca was a long forgotten mission, she hope for another century. The wait seemed long for their special eve and they became jittery, Josina had several attempts to find her book and other belongings, Avoca though did not need a book for her findings and knowledge, she found she had a gift and everything she saw and learnt she was storing away in her mind, one day she would record her findings for little Agnes for now though she would carry them safely in her head. Avoca hated this time she often smelt foul smoke and heard screams, this only reminded her of her own loss and more. Danger was all around them and they would do well not to be caught, she begged Josina to give up on her book hunt in fear she would be captured, Josina though had no fear and carried on her search each time she would bring back books and treasure, one day she bought back a book that Avoca recognised it was large and had a special clasp, she had seen it as a child long ago an old lady held it near a fire and she chanted its words, her mother had said she was her great Grandmother and the book would fall to her one day, the book was written in Sanskrit a language she knew, Josina had no interest and was glad Avoca liked her book, Josina never realised the power she had handed her friend and Avoca did not realise at first, until she started to practise some of the spells and realised the book gave her the knowledge of a very powerful witch, this gave her more hope of escaping and finding Agnes. Josina and Avoca one day decided to find supplies in the village they needed spice and produce they could not forage for in the forest for their spells. They wrapped themselves up well and keeping their heads down walked around the little market, gathering what they needed, Josina had plenty of coins from her thieving, as they approached one small stall Josina saw a little girl much like Agnes, she sat on a stool as her Mother sold spice and dried leaves, this by chance was just the stall the witches needed, Josina knew straight away it was her book the little girl studied and thought how to trick it from the girl without suspicion and a scene, Avoca saw also and began nervously to choose their needed spices, the girl was absorbed by the book and ran her little fingers over the words and symbols, the market grew busier as people came from the mountains and soon the little stall was over run, Avoca bought their goods and turned to see both Josina and the girl were gone, at first Avoca panicked worried that something had happened to Josina, she then realised something had happened to the little girl, quickly Avoca disappeared into the crowd and was soon in the safety of the forest, she had not walked far, when Josina appeared gloating from behind some trees, holding her treasured book, Avoca was pleased for her and enquired where the little girl was, she need not have asked for stood behind her the poor thing stood shaking, shocked Avoca asked Josina what they were to do with the child, she would tell surely and they would be captured, Josina agreed and they took the little girl with them to their cave, her name was Preeti and once she had stop crying, she seemed intrigued and watched closely when the witches made potions or pastes, she ate well and slept well, Preeti was clever she knew not to cause trouble or her captors could turn on her, instead she was sweet and helpful, the witches enjoyed her company and taught her skills in making potions, Preeti would read their books and remember so much, she began to consider this her opportunity to escape the village, her future and arranged marriage with the fat pig called Rahul, she hated him in every way imaginable he was cruel, greedy and arrogant; yet her father said he was a good match and she would want for nothing. So Preeti stayed hidden in the cave, more than once she had the chance to escape and heard voices of villagers, she stayed hidden though and even warned the witches when she heard village people. Avoca grew found of the girl and would be sad to take her back to the village, one evening Preeti heard them talking of going and how they would leave Preeti outside the village, Preeti immediately begged them not to take her back and when she understood she could not go with them she made them vow to take her to the Fort, where she could peddle potions for her keep and that way she would be free, the witches agreed and so the plan was put in place and on the night of Samhain, the witches took her well prepared with everything she would need, they packed themselves and hid their cave, they returned to the Fort and saw sweet Preeti walk in through the huge doors before nightfall. Preeti was amazed when she walked into the fortress it was a hub of activity she was enthralled from the moment she arrived; she never noticed the flame of light outside fortress walls. Preeti quickly found herself simple lodgings in a room above the stables and paid in advance for a year with her jewels from the witches, she hid her other jewels and books and cleaned her new abode, she then set herself up lighting the small fire for cooking, by morning Preeti had enough potions to sell and soon she was happily curing and caring for the poor of the Fort, word spread and she was summoned to the wealthy, Preeti became a popular healer. The Fort was now a settled place under a different ruler, Preeti did not lack admirers, however Preeti did not wished to be tied down and saw another plan, for the witches had not been as clever as they thought. Preeti had hidden well during those months of captivity that she herself was born under a black moon and although the villagers called her cursed, Preeti called it a blessing and she knew from a small child that she was different somehow and by luck or by chance that day the witches stole her they showed her the way. Preeti now had a life of freedom forever.

THE LORD VISITS

Avia had not seen her father for months, he had been on some archeology dig somewhere, he came back less and less and sometimes he failed to even see the girls, this time was different, he came back unannounced, much to Miss Bonneville's horror, he was pleased with the house and complimented her on how wonderful everything was, he met the new staff including the seamstress, he marvelled at her wonderful work and then went to find his children, Lord Richard Hoare did not even think they would miss him or notice him gone, so he breezily walked into their parlour, as if it was a normal occurrence, the girls were shocked and were glad they had had guests earlier as they were all well dressed and turned out. Cecilia greeted him with joy followed by her sisters, Avia was a little unsure he had never been very receptive towards her, this time though he looked as though a black cloud had lifted from his brows, he listened to their interesting visit to Bath, Cecilia told him of her fashionable invitations and Olivia of her friendship with Thomas and Edwina, Avia had little to say, so she went to get her book and showed him her own sketches and told him of her garden, she was thrilled, as he said he would visit it, the very next day, later they all sat and had dinner together and he gave them each a velvet necklace with a pretty cameo for their parties, they all agreed it had been a perfect day. Earlier that day Avia had sat with Jack on the stone bench outside the cottage she had shown him her book and he marvelled at the drawings and information, Avia said he could looked at it whenever he wished too. Both Jack and Avia felt safer in the gardens since their rushed meeting with Agnes after the trip to Bath, they had taken down all the strange charms and buried them, replacing them with cross's made from straw, Agnes had sprinkled a concoction she made around the garden and cottage and mumbled a rhyme, while Jack and Avia had planted St Johns Wart and Hellebore to keep evil out, they all agreed though they should only be there in company. Agnes was told Belle's story and they knew it was only matter of time until the witches would return. Jack and Avia after looking at the book tended to the garden and talked about Agnes, they wonder if she could stay and they worried for her, they knew Agnes did not want to be a taken witch and was happy as she was. The following day was bright and Avia's father as promised was waiting for her in the hall way they walked briskly to the Gothic cottage, as her father told her interesting historical facts about the garden, statues and temples, Avia listened with interest and was so excited to show him her creation, when they arrived Jack of course was there and Avia worried her Father would be cross, he instead greeted him in an very pleasant way, Jack politely introduced himself as Belle and Jeremiah's son from Stourton Farm, Avia's father had not realised he gardened for them and seemed pleased saying how found he was of Belle and how she had been Octavia's Mother's dresser. He summed Jack up and said he thought one day he would be head gardener at Stourton, Jack smiled and said he would like that very much. Lord Richard then drew his attention to his daughters creation and was clearly pleased by the clever planting and introduction of a small pond, fountain and a wonderful gazebo, he complimented her on her roses and topiary and loved how she had planted hellebores gently all around the garden drifting into the woods, Jack and Avia smiled at each other pleased and also thankful her Father did not realise they did more than look pretty, they circled the garden and cottage with a spell to keep out witches or any other unwanted visitor's, Lord Richard then chatted about the gardens of Stourton Hall and he looked at his daughter with great pride, saying she was like her Great Grandfather Henry the magnificent. Avia felt so pleased she felt she was flying and dared to hug her father in glee and from that day on something changed for Avia and her father, they had something to talk about, so when ever he was not to busy, he would walk with her and tell her all he knew about the wonderful history of the gardens and his plans and desires for the place, he invited Avia to help and was impressed with her drawings and ideas, Lord Richard saw Avia as his knew partner in such matters. Avia and Jack met again later that day and were pleased to see Agnes join them with her companion Hestia the large mysterious cat, the three of them carried on fixing their circle planting of St Johns Wort and the scattering of lodestones they had found in the cavern, they then sat making more straw crosses and although they spent most of their time protecting the garden now, they still played and had fun. The summer months spun a head giving them chance to explore and enjoy lovely long evenings together, Avia could hardly believe that soon it would be a year since she had found her two best friends in the garden, Jack and Agnes, Agnes did so well in her work and her dress's had been the talk of the season, she had refused a lot of work from requests even with a little magic she could not convincingly make to many without suspicion. Avia wished this summer could last forever it felt perfect everything was in place, she felt as though she did not have a care in the world. Yet around the corner autumn would soon knock on their doors and something brewed in the stars and the moon had an eerie orange glow, sorcery had begun and nothing now could stop the future and forces that would collide and threaten Avia's summer of long content.

CHITRAKUT FORT ON SAMHAIN 1304

Avoca and Josina had watched Preeti disappear through the gates to what they now considered hell, for Preeti though they knew it was safe. The witches had their own job to do and although Avoca would miss Preeti she had her own daughter to find, they had decide to try and land in Stourton woods a hundred years on from when they left. This was the first time they had made it back, since leaving little Agnes, they saw great change a lot of woodland had disappeared and acres of sheep grazed in its place. Josina and Avoca stayed at the cottage in 1508 for a whole year searching for Agnes, the land must have shifted though something had changed and Agnes and her cavern could not be found, for some strange reason it stayed hidden, still the Yew tree stood there holding its deep dark secret, their months at Stourton wood were mischievous, they made its their home no one seemed to notice them and they thieved and caused jiggery-pokery where ever they went, instead of peddling and becoming known for their potions, like ghosts in the night they would trick, steal and vanish. If they found a young girl wandering in their domain they would keep her until they left enjoying the company of a child, who they felt they were teaching a great skill, some would return home when they were gone, others though would ask for freedom like Preeti and sadly a couple would die of a mistaken over dose of potion, Josina told Avoca that their hearts were weak and they would have died what ever path they had taken, Josina though knew they would tell the village and castle of their existence, so with a pleasant tasting cinnamon poison she would let them go to a peaceful place. In the year 1794 when the witches returned yet again, tired of the world they wished to rest at Stourton woods, yet more had change the castle was gone and lakes and flowers adorned the gentle land, once full of ancient woods, they were thankful the stone cottage still lay hidden in the woods, the witches had arrived early on that day, a time difference in the hemisphere and light was an unwelcome outcome, they however settled in planning a quiet All Hallows Eve with no guests, they had met Parnell, Wilmot and Lettice in another time at the chateau in France, holding meetings with the warlock. So Josina and Avoca planned a quiet night for witches on the eve of Samhain. The earth was colder than they had ever known on that night and the frost played tricks in the woods, the glistening white frost lead a girl of high birth with an elegant face called Belle far off her path, it drew her in whispers to the cottage door, as if in a trance by her fear she knocked on their door. Josina knew immediately that she was of no use to them, she was from the grand Hall where the castle once stood and she walked from the land that was sculptured into a painting, Josina looked her up and down and thought of Fabian her friend the warlock, he had lost his house keeper and this girl of high birth would make him a lovely gift. The Belle girl was dangerous though so Josina gave her the poison whilst deciding what to do, they walked her to a path where no one would find her for days and they would be gone, Josina though thought to take her to the master warlock as a pawn that may win her some favour. Avoca ignorant of her friends plans just thought her sleepy and that she would just wake a little cold. Had it not been for the boy with the whistling tune and a little panic, Belle would have been lost forever to the warlock. For Belle though she was twice lucky, the witch Josina in her haste had made a mistake and added more parsley instead of more hemlock, the girl was poorly enough but not nearly dead and had the boy not come a long she would be a warlocks housekeeper. Josina knew it was to risky to fly, so quickly left her frail body and her and Avoca ran back to the cottage, they had vanished before they saw Belle being saved and Josina never believed she would have lived on without the warlocks magic.

1810 BACK TO STOURTON BY STONES

After that evening in 1794 the witches had not been back to Stourton, worried they were becoming to well known, through the centuries stories had gathered about the witches in the woods, Josina said this was their last chance to find Agnes, she had to land them in the right year and had practiced until she had perfected her spell, Avoca had a strong feeling that something had happened and Agnes needed their help, so although hesitant to return as they had had so many failed attempts, she agreed as she always did with her friend Josina. As they lit their fire on the Samhain night and prepared to travel they knew they would not be alone, others gathered to join them they could see it in the stars and something else was happening that Avoca was not sure about, the moon turn to red and the skies orange, a warm wind blew in spirits from a far, Josina seemed nervous and unlike herself as though she prepared for something huge, Avoca felt worried and thought perhaps they could stay another year, the cave wasn't to bad and she could visit Preeti, Josina held her firm though and whispered the words, the fire and winds grew and the time had come. Josina and Avoca landed in a rather ungainly fashion thankfully alone, they knew for certain they had been thrown off course by something and instead of the sweet oak woods of Stourton, they found themselves on a grassland plain that stretch for miles its gradient went up and down like a blanket blowing in the wind, in the distance they could see several fires in a ring and the flash of lights as others arrived like them, the harsh wind buffeted them as they walked frustrated and fed up, Josina broke all the rules and with Avoca's hand in a tight grip she produce the feather of a buzzard and said her spell, with great speed they flew cutting through the crisp night air landing not far from the strange spectacle, Josina knew she was at the place of sacrifice a ring of stones stood, the huge stones were very ancient and were Sarsen and Bluestone, the site was a place used through the ages for burials and other ceremonies and for years the witches had gathered here to celebrate Samhain Eve, it was told with the sun and the moon you could read the future from the circle of stones, Avoca had never heard of this place before and although this was not their plan, she saw no harm in following Josina and having a little look at their fellow witches celebrate the evening. As they came closer she realised this was no normal gathering and began to think it a mistake and hung back and watched from a far hidden by the shadows, Josina then saw Parnell and Wilmot surely they had not been knocked off course too, cautiously they went towards the stones gently calling their friends Wilmot immediately turned and soon they were huddle together, greeting each other, each one as bemused as the other as to why they had landed here and not Stourton woods, they wondered where poor Lettice had landed, as she did not turn up and decided to make their way by flight to the woods, maybe Lettice had made it. Eventually they found the woods and walked towards the cottage, they were soon intercepted by a very cross Lettice asking where they had been, complaining her perfect stew was drying, they followed her, not to the cottage but to an old wooden shed they presumed abandoned by a wood cutter by the amount of saw dust, axes and saws, Lettice bid them to sit by the fire and she served her meal, as though they were sat around an grand dinning table, after their food Lettice began her tale. Lettice said she had got in a muddle and arrived the year before and only realised her mistake when it was to late to travel back, so she had stayed in the woods, the cottage though was not safe a garden had been made and a girl and a boy were always there; then she held

Avoca's hand and told her somehow Agnes had got out of her wooden chest and cavern and walked the earth, the witches gasped how could this be and Lettice told all she knew from her eaves dropping and spying. The witches did not understand quite how she had been able to get out alone, had another witch broken the spell, what ever had happened, Avoca needed to see Agnes and take her far away, Josina reminded her she would still be far to young to go through the port holes, Avoca though said they could travel abroad. Lettice thought she had been taken as a serf to work in the castle, she said everything looked different though a lot had changed, she thought she could get to Agnes through the girl who was always in the garden, Lettice said of late though she had never been alone and was always with the boy, then she told them about the charms in the tree and the planting circle and stones. Josina was clever and quick she knew Agnes had done this and she feared Avoca would become suspicious, so kept it to herself, four hundred years was along time to leave someone under the ground and although she would be the same age, Josina knew it was to long, she would think of the first people she met as her family, Agnes was no longer theirs to take, Josina though would go along with Avoca, she feared now that Avoca would see their plan, it was no mistake that the witches and warlocks from far and wide gathered at the strange circle of stones, the year 1810 was the year of the warlocks greatest plan.

BELLE AND THE COULDRON

Belle felt very twitchy on every All Hallows Eve's, this particular one she felt it even more nervous than ever, there was a strange orange glow to the moon, strange howls could be heard faintly and a stale smell stifled the normal fresh air. Stourton Hall were having a bonfire party and all had been invited, Belle looked forward to seeing her friends and with Jeremiah, Bertie and Jack by her side she should have felt no fear, as they walked through the woods, a cruel wind blew from the east carrying upon it a sinister secret and still that strange pungent smell, Belle could not quite put her mind to it as they walked deeper into the wood, the smell grew stronger and even the men committed on its strange aroma, they saw a trickle of smoke through the trees, Jeremiah said he would investigate as he knew since old Mac's death, no one had lived in the wood cutters shack. Belle felt uncertain and begged they carry on claiming it would be rude to be late, Jeremiah though insisted, he protested a fire out of someones watch could be dangerous, reluctantly Belle followed as they approached the shack she instantly recognised the aroma and above the little fire a cauldron hung, no one was there, Bella knew though that the witches were back. Jeremiah puzzled, put out the fire he tipped the cauldron and closed up the shack, he would send the gamekeeper Otto and some men out the following day, Jeremiah saw his distraught wife and knew, he remembered himself that night so long ago, the strange feeling of fear and the ghastly smell in the woods that night, just before he found Belle just lying there near to death and now all those years on that same smell and sense of fear drifted through the woods, he held Belle and bid the boys to make haste, they would try to pick up the lane and stay at the Hall that night, Belle felt such panic and walked as fast as she could manage, the witches were back she knew it and she knew they came for Agnes, she had to reach Avia and Agnes as fast as possible, the wooded paths seemed to take forever and the darkness grew, roots and stones tripped their feet and branches lashed in their way, Jeremiah had them all link arms to keep each one safe, they had to get out of the woods as fast as they could. Never had Belle been so relieved to make it to the Hall, they scampered up the gravel drive and joined the others who gathered in the stable yard protected by its walls, at last they felt they could breath, Bertie asked what was going on, he was cut short though by Belle who told Jack to get Avia and fast. Avia and Agnes were safely all wrapped up warm in the Hall, they stood in the library with its huge windows from there they could see the fire and watch everyone, Cecilia and Olivia were staying at Dyrham Park with Edwina, Thomas's sister, they were attending a lavish party. Avia had asked permission that she could watch the bonfire with Agnes and it was agreed as the East wind was so biting they could watch from inside, Miss Bonneville didn't want the cold air or smoke on Avia's chest. Jack arrived at the hall and asked if he could relay a message to Miss Octavia from his mother Belle of a personal nature, trusted by the butler Arthur he was escorted to the library, Avia and Agnes could not quite believe it when they saw Jack and excitedly chatted and offered him little cakes and cordial they had been given for the occasion. Jack stood with them looking over the lawns and the bonfire, that burnt away from any buildings, he saw all the villagers and Hall staff gather with jugs of ale or spirits, music was played and some danced with joy. Jack was so relieved to see them safely inside and once the main glow of the fire had died, he told them of their findings in the woods and how Belle and Jeremiah had reacted, he told them of the fire and the cauldron and the strange smell and whispered to them both that Belle had mumbled, their back, the witches are back. Agnes knew they were here herself she had felt their presence, she could almost see them so powerful were her thoughts, several times over the last few months she had sworn she had seen someone in the woods and seen small fires. One day she had followed a young fallow deer so amazed by its pretty markings and sweetness, her path took her deep into the woods and she saw the image of someone she once knew, Agnes hid quickly flying up a tree and watched her as she passed from above, there was no mistaking that it was Lettice and that meant the others would follow, Agnes remembered she used to like Lettice and her funny ways and many dress's, now she felt nothing but contempt and fear, Agnes did not follow her and fled back to the safety of the Hall, when Agnes heard Belle's story and remembered her own life before she felt so much anger. She listened carefully to Jack whilst she stood in the amazing library near her dearest friend and she began to feel confused, she hadn't decided the best way to react if her so called mother ever came back, Agnes asked Avia if they could speak with Belle. By this time Jeremiah had put out word that there was trouble in the woods he did not use the word witches, enough fear was stirred to warn folk to stay clear though and that night they would all stay above the stables and in the barns, when Jack came and asked Belle to join them in the library she was grateful to get out of the cold and after telling her husband, she went with Jack, Arthur greeted her with kindness and with the Lord of the Hall else where and the sisters away he saw no harm and arranged for warm wine to be sent for Belle with bread and cheese, the four of them sat in the library watching the embers of the fire and each told their account of what they had seen and of what they each thought, all decided they would sleep on their thoughts if they could and Belle was invited to stay in the house by Avia, she felt awful as she sent poor Jack to the stables and cold, Avia walked through the halls long rooms with Jack for a little while whilst Agnes and Belle went to the servants quarters, Avia wanted to know Jacks thoughts, Avia was quite shocked and surprisingly pleased by his answer, firstly he thought Agnes should meet her mother and send her away, he thought her strong enough and thought she hid her witch side well and should stay at the Hall. Jack also said though he would not like Avia any where near any of it and he made her promise to stay in the Hall and then he said the words that she did not expect from someone so young, he said he cared for her and wanted her safe and didn't no what he would do if something happened to her, he was scared the witches might want to take her, they had taken others before, Jack stood there with tears near his eyes and said goodnight to Miss Avia. Avia ran to her room as soon as he had gone, she was a bag of nerves and could never sleep, with witches running wild in the woods and having Belle to stay and thinking of Agnes with her dilemma and herself just mulling over and over again that Jack cared for her. Avia was the most terrified and most gratified anyone could be. Avia checked she had her moonstone necklace and bracelet firmly on, she found her poetry book she had been given by her Father that came all the way from India, the poems were said to be ancient from Indian folk lore and were translated to English with pretty flowers drawings, she read her favourite poems and recited the one she always sang when gardening or when trying to calm her nerves.

The rivers and ponds flow flowers up to the moon,
The trees like dancers glow with blossom in full bloom,
The mango fruits sweet and perfumed send orange
to the skies,
The birds and the bees sing songs of joyous times,
With delighted everlasting howls and cries,
The magical swans and peaceful turtle dove,
Trust to carry on with a forever secret lasting love,
So set free the little caged bird deep in the ground
let it flutter and fly,
Sing the tune of joy little bird for freedom you can
once again cry.

A TRICK OF A WITCH

Agnes before she went to bed that night asked Miss Bonneville to make doubly sure that all the servants kept windows and doors locked, gossip had already reached everyone though and suspicious talk of strange happenings in the woods of Stourton had everyone locked up in their rooms, to ride out the night of All Hallows Eve. Agnes could not sleep and went to see Avia, she crept along the corridors in the dark afraid to light a candle, she did not want to be seen, as she approached Avia's room she heard her singing her poem, the poem she sang when she was gardening and the poem she sang on the day Agnes was set free, when she went into her room she saw the moonstone around Agnes's neck a memory flashed back to her and suddenly everything made sense. Agnes sat with Avia and spoke to her, the poem was ancient and although her Mother had spoken it in another language, it was the poem that set her free, Agnes declared Avia had performed a spell bye some miracle, she had been able to set her free, she then asked her about the moonstone necklace again, Avia said she had found it, Agnes had already confirmed it was not hers, she had never seen it before, then they thought of all the treasures they had found in the cavern, now hidden in the cottage, they decided it was probably stolen by the witches, the moonstone glittered and glowed as if it knew it was been talked about, Agnes eyed it suspiciously and asked if she could look at it, promising she would give it back, Avia reluctantly agreed and Agnes studied the necklace she found engravings of tiny symbols on the back, from memory of her Mothers teachings, she knew that it meant it was a protection stone, Agnes though did not know what from she felt certain though it would be witches. Agnes then said in the morning she was going to find the witches and speak to her Mother and ask them kindly to go away, Avia was worried she didn't think it was safe, what if they took her, no one would be able to rescue her. Agnes sat on Avia's bed as they wondered what to, both exhausted they drifted off to sleep, Agnes dreamt of witches flying over the Hall and sweeping down trying to find away in, she could see them clearly and heard them call her name. Agnes's dream was really happening for outside the witches had gathered while everyone slept, they prowled around and at last they found her, first they tried to get through the windows with no joy, then they saw the huge smokeless chimney pots some with broken tops, it was not long before they were in and dusting of old soot and birds nests. Lettice stayed behind afraid her physic would not quite fit the narrow chimney pots. Once in the huge library they knew which way to turn and soon they were outside the room of the sleeping girls, so quietly they crept in. Avoca saw her little Agnes lying there holding the other girls hand so sweet and delicate both of them, Agnes shone and looked so neat, unlike the Agnes she had left, the sleeping girls held hands and the witches gently reached for Agnes to carry her away, suddenly they were thrown by some power straight across the room the thud of their witch bodies woke the sleeping girls, who screamed and clung to each other, Hestia pounced from nowhere she hissed and growled at the witches, shocked to see her back they were a little stunned, then Josina saw the sacred moonstone. The witches started tutting and cursing their plan so simple had started to go wrong. Agnes realising the gemstone had worked, decided to take this strange and terrifying opportunity to have a little word, she recognised her Mother and stared at her with hate and asked how could she have left her for four hundred years, in a chest under ground, Avoca tried hard to explain, Agnes said bitterly she would never go with them, her home was here in the Hall. Avoca was shocked and felt so very sad, Josina though was angry and started to make a spell and Agnes did not know how but she began to make one as well. Avoca started saying it was fine, they would all just leave and hoped she could just see Agnes before she went away. The other witches unknown to Avoca though had a sinister plan to catch the young witch born of a witch and warlock and take her to the stones, where she would be a sacrifice for a greater cause, giving all the witches more power and immortality than ever before. Avoca suddenly realised reading Josina's mind that she planned a ritual of horror, desperate to save Agnes and the other girl she had to come up with something quickly, then she thought of her little Agnes and the little tricks she had played, from the spells she had learnt, her favourite was always to disappear from sight, Avoca praying she would remember said the rhyme that Agnes would finish and the spell was fixed. Agnes had vanished into thin air the witches sniffed and prodded, then Josina screamed that they would take the other girl to deceive the other witches and war-locks, they had promised to bring the child. Agnes still held the moonstone pendant and without any hesitation Avia was whisked away. Avoca begged them to let her go, Josina cackled with the others she was a fool, they had no choice a packed had been made the moon and stars were aligned, this eve would not happen for another thousand years, the child would do the trick the other witches would never know until they died. Avoca sobbed and realised they had planned this all along ago, she felt so cross and foolish, Josina her friend had been up to chicanery for years, everything she had done was to make Avoca have a little witch from a warlock for this year as a sacrifice. All her secret trips and introductions now made perfect sense. Agnes may have disappeared but she heard every word and she listened with hor-ror to the plan that had been made. Agnes fought back tears as she realised why she had been created and what they wanted her for and then she started to feel anger rage inside her, they would not take Avia, she would rather die herself, Agnes heard Avoca's use-less plea to leave, Josina, Wilmot and Parnell had no intentions of listening to anyone though, they had planned this for hundreds of years and Avoca had fallen into every trap and plan they had made, it was no coincidence her father had sold her all those years ago, or that she had a child with the alchemist or warlock, or that she was hunted so she would have to leave Agnes, they needed Agnes to be ten years old on the Samhain Eve of 1810. Poor Avoca had no clue she thought of her life and how since meeting Josina, Josina had controlled so much and taken her to so many places and left her when it suited her, she thought how she helped her kill the alchemist, everything was leading all the time to this date. Agnes her sweet little witch was to be a sacrifice, she could not bare for either girls to die and she knew clever Josina would take them both if she could, Avoca had to think quickly she had so many powers she had hidden from Josina over the years she had read and learnt so much, just as Agnes reappeared quickly grabbing hold of Avia so she still had protection, Josina made a final attempt to grab Agnes and Avoca cast her spell.

AWAY IN A MANGER

Jack his brother and Father had an uncomfortable night lying in the wooden feeding mangers for the horses, Each time they moved they shuddered with cold and winced with an ache, they thought of what was out in those woods and settled back down feeling safe in the courtyard of the stable with the dogs and game keeper and his gun about. A lot of the villagers had stayed not wanting to risk the walk, so they still heard whispers of those who choose to keep sleep from their heads. Jack kept waking and he had an over whelming sense that something was very wrong, he would each time though fade back into a disturbed sleep, each time in his dreams he saw Miss Avia, this time though he saw her vividly floating in a manger in the lake, the cold waters surrounding her and she was still and pale, Jack woke with a shudder, terrified his dream was true he ran from the stable barn towards the lake, the moon lit his way and although scared he had to see if she was there, he looked over the lake nothing was there as he looked over towards where the cottage lay he saw a flicker of light, with all his haste he ran stumbling at times towards the cottage, as he ran he screamed for help in hope someone would hear his cries, Jack never really knew how he knew that Avia had been taken from her bed, as he ran towards the Gothic cottage, he saw her lying there so still as she was in his dream, only she was laid by a small fire that flickered suspiciously with no fuel, the icy ground was so cold, with no hesitation he threw his jacket over her and lifted her from the ground and ran, from the corner of his eye he saw the witches, his mind thought of Agnes should he have stayed and looked for her, Jack carried on running though others could come back and search for Agnes she had more chance of survival, Avia was cold and hardly breathed as he ran to the top path, a group of men came towards him, his Father and brother among them, he asked them to go to the cottage and looked for Agnes and Jack kept running, he banged loudly on the kitchen doors to the great Hall, Miss Bonneville was there in seconds as if she waited for his knock, they quickly got Avia to the kitchen where the range chugged the nights and days away keeping the kitchen warm, they popped her in cooks cosy chair and covered her with blankets, Miss Bonnevillle tried to wake her as gently as she could and slowly Miss Avia came around, sobbing she asked for Agnes, Miss Bonneville and Jack comforted her and she was given warm herb flavoured milk and honey, Jack held her cold hands and asked if she knew where they had gone, Avia sobbed she had no clue and said there was nothing they could do and she mumbled about a plan and how they were always going to take her little Agnes away. Avia was terrified and with her sisters and Father away and Nanny Maud ill in bed with a fever, she was kept with the servants, Belle came down to comfort her and they all sat huddled in the warm kitchen, waiting for the dawn to come and praying for Agnes nothing else could be done.

SPLIT BY A SCRAPE

Avoca's spell had worked with in seconds her and Agnes and Avia were by the cottage, only Avia in shock lay still as if she was dead, Agnes screamed to see her friend look so ill, Avoca quickly gave her a warming potion and lit a fire with spells, she pleaded with Agnes they had no time, Josina and the others would be with them in minutes and she was not strong enough to fight them all. All those days from being in the cave with Preeti paid of that night, for when Josina went about her dealings, Avoca learnt like Preeti everything she could and she had read Josina's precious book of time, she understood how to use it and one time and place she had memorised was the time of the cave and sweet Preeti who they had stolen, Avoca knew she had to get back to Preeti to warn her and to save her precious Agnes, because she now knew both were in danger and Preeti would have no warning. Poor Agnes did not want to go she cried to let her stay she understood though the witches would not let her go and their plan was not a good one, Agnes quickly put the moonstone around Avia's neck, she kissed her on the forehead and whispered she would be back, Agnes and Avoca were gone all they left was glitter in the sky. Josina and the others arrived at the cottage they flew around looking for Agnes and Avoca and screeched with frustration so annoyed by their escape. The witches saw the little girl just lying there by Avoca's fire, they just had to get the moonstone from her neck and she was theirs, Hestia appeared and pounced and prowled around scratching at the witches, each time they callously shoved her away. Lettice got a little stick knowing the necklace would burn her hands badly, she stood from a distance and with magic she threaded it through the chain and was about to yank it, when she was thrown by a boy who appeared from nowhere, he grabbed the girl so quickly and ran. The witches heard other voices and lights and dogs barking. Both the girl and Agnes were gone and now the witch hunt had begun, the sherif had been called a search was on. The witches were defeated and Josina knew she had lost, she could not return to the stones and she had less strength these days, she had needed the power of the sacrifice, Josina like lightning had a thought and with the other witches they had a quick trip to an-other land, just one last chance to solve their dilemma, the hours of the night were going fast if quick though they would just make it back in time.

QUICK STICKS,TURN AROUND

Avoca and Agnes landed out side the Fort of Chitrakut just where they had left, Avoca knew Agnes was exhausted and confused, but she had to follow quickly, they had to find Preeti if they were to go back to the Hall, Agnes obeyed and listened realising it was her only hope, they easily got into the Fort without anyone seeing them through an old damp tunnel Avoca remembered they quickly looked for Preeti, Avoca prayed she was not far, the streets bustled with wonderful colours and aromas of the bazaar, Avoca saw her immediately just as she had thought she had a small stall and sold her potions as Avoca had done with Agnes once, Preeti was shocked to see Avoca back so soon and she saw the distressed little Agnes and gave her a tonic, Preeti knew who she was straight away, Avoca had told her she had a daughter she had to find, Avoca did not waste time she told her quietly of Josina's plan and asked how they could protect Agnes.

Preeti quickly packed away her stall and lead them back to her rooms, she lit her fire asking Avoca how she thought she could help. Avoca said she knew she was a witch herself she could see it in the caves and she knew she had powers much stronger than Avoca's or Agnes's, Avoca told her she had worked out she was born under a black moon. Preeti smiled and agreed she had grown stronger and more powerful and with each day she learnt and set her mind to things. Avoca told Preeti she thought Josina and her coven planned to take her instead she was a perfect fit for Josina and her disastrous plan. Preeti acted quickly she didn't need any second warnings she knew from the start Josina was not kind like

Avoca. In Preeti's possession she had lots of pretty charm stones she sold, each had different meaning she took three black shiny stones with white dots, Preeti then put each little stone into the fire with other powder, she carefully took them out and welded chains around the stones she placed a bracelet on both of their wrists and then performed another spell Agnes could feel the heat burn her wrist, Preeti comforted her the pain would pass quickly, but the burn would stay deep in her skin, the stone of Obsidian would always protector her from any spiritual force, the bracelet was impossible to remove unless by magic she would most certainly be safe now from witches and warlocks. Avoca spoke to Agnes and told her what they had to do and that they only had a little time left, Preeti gifted Agnes another charm on a pendant for her friend Avia, she said the little rose quartz would help her heal and give her love and protection. The three witches with capes pulled around them walked back through the tunnel and out onto the hill, Avoca had written a note and wrapped Agnes's birthstone in it, she gave both to Agnes and said she loved her with all her heart, but they could not live as Agnes wished together, she said one day when it was safe she would visit again and if she needed her she would be back here with Preeti. Avoca told Agnes exactly what to say and gave her the potions to throw to the skies with a couple of minutes left she was gone, then Preeti and Avoca did the same ritual and disappeared. Josina, Wilmot, Parnell and Lettice all arrived at the Fort, Josina knew exactly where she lived and held her little stall, they would be able to find Preeti with complete ease and the sweet natured child would have no clue, so trusting and obedient unlike Agnes, they ignored stares and comments and not seeing her stall ran straight to her rooms. Preeti was gone, Josina screeched again to hurry they had no time and as the huge shadows grew over the moon and the wind blew dust from the sands that before had stood still, Josina and her coven realised their fate, the hour had past and they were stuck here in the fort with onlookers and guards, each witch held their defence and with magical force stopped their arrest the word Dayan could be heard. They began their escape and all but poor Lettice made it out, she was to slow her cries could be heard Josina though had no thought for a rescue mission tonight, she was the hunted instead of the hunter, with a weakness setting in and others in the witch world after her, she needed to lay low. She would not hang around to see Lettice's fate, Josina felt cursed and cared for no one but herself, so she ran and intended to disappear off the face of the sorry earth, everything was ruined, she felt vengeful though towards that annoying little witch Agnes and Avoca who had turned and betrayed her, to hunt them though she had no strength. Wilmot and Parnell were also fuming they had wanted to go home to their lovely lakeside home, now they were stuck in this hot unknown land for a year with dwindling health, they parted company from Josina on bad terms after all those years of their alliance and planning, everything now seemed a waste of time they had lost immortality and power beyond even their belief, the ancient scriptures Fabian the warlock had read clearly claimed that these amazing prodigies could only take place in a perfect storm of events and although witches could live for a very long time, they knew their time on earth was not for ever as they wished.

PREETI AND AVOKA

Preeti and Avoca landed with a bump back outside the walls of the Fort they both felt a little dizzy and Avoca was now very weary and felt sad inside and empty. Preeti was sad for her friend she was also glad of her friendship and her warning, Avoca knew that the witches would be here somewhere, she knew they were to late for their sacrifices and with thousands of years to wait Preeti or Agnes could no longer be their victims. Preeti was now very powerful they would not dare to try and take her and Avoca on, Agnes had also gifted her a present that would give her more strength and life, a simple kiss and spell of life love. Preeti and Avoca returned to the rooms and Preeti made up a bed for Avoca and gave her food and drink, they then slept deeply with no fear, when Avoca woke the next morning late to the sound of prayers, for the first time in her life she felt free and although sad to loose Agnes, she knew she would find contentment here in the Fort walls and have a good life, she would make her life with Preeti, she ate the flat bread and olives and drank the warm goats milk, she washed and changed into some clothes of Preeti's and went out into the dazzling sunshine and bazaar, she found Preeti smiling and admiring her outfit with laughter and Avoca became her wise assistant, they lied to others saying she was her Mother who was now widowed. Avoca and Preeti soon moved to a pretty stone house in the walls of the fort, they had a roof garden and lots of room to make their potions and live happily. One day not long after they had moved they heard lots of noise and jeering coming from the gathering crowds, with curiosity they walked to the centre of the Fort and in the huge court raised on four stakes they saw to their horror Josina, Parnell, Wilmot and Lettice in a sad and sorry state, how they had been hunted down Avoca could not think, she and Preeti disappeared from view, they did not want too see what happened, Avoca half thought to rescue them, but she could not risk Preeti's life and hers and why would she save the witches, who had ruined her life and nearly killed her own daughter and Avia her best friend. Avoca would not watch, she would know though that they were gone and some justice had been served for all the tricks and murders the coven had played on its way through the centuries. Avoca could not understand how they had been caught all were so quick and clever and they were powerful witches, Avoca couldn't help thinking it was punishment from others of their type, after their disastrous evening , a lot of witches and warlocks had gathered on that All Hallows Eve at the stones, she was glad they had never seen Agnes or Avoca and she had stayed hidden from view, maybe they would have her name though, so she decided to call herself Petra. Both would have to be careful, they set themselves up as alchemist hiding any sign of spells. The next day Avoca heard something very strange had happened, apparently the witches had just vanished into thin air. Avoca looked as shocked and aghast as everyone else and later she looked at the dates, it was the first equinox of the year and not an uncommon time for a desperate witch to travel on such a day, it certainly came with risks of landing in a completely wrong time and place, they had no choice though Avoca felt uneasy that they were still on the earth, Preeti reassured her though that they were all safe, she said she doubted though Josina and the others were, they were hunted and on the run.

BACK WITH A BUMP

Agnes landed back at the Gothic cottage with a huge bump, she crashed into her friend the yew tree and fell to the ground, Avia was gone and for this moment in time she did not know if this was good or bad, the night was bitterly cold and the skies were clear, she sat for a few moments trying to digest all that had happened, she felt a panic though, what if they had managed to take Avia she didn't know which way to turn, she was about to somehow take flight and go towards the stones, thinking maybe she could save her, praying it wasn't to late Agnes stood only to fall into a bush, dizzy from her catapult through time, for Agnes this was a lucky fall the last place Agnes needed to be was by the ancient stones and had she taken to flight, she would have instantly been spotted, witches flew searching in the skies for their lost coven of witches and child sacrifice, Agnes still reeling looked to the sky, she saw shadows of many witches flickering through the trees, she quickly hid in the cover of the yew tree and in her mind she whispered many protection spells over an over again, Hestia appeared purring and rubbing her head against Agnes's arm, appreciating her return, Agnes fused her comforted by her presence, although still scared she didn't know Josina and the others were far away, she just kept saying her chants and clinging to her charm that Preeti had gifted her, Agnes still felt the soreness of the burn, she felt a strong reassurance of safety from the bracelet stone though and then she heard shouting and dogs barking and she knew they came for her, she saw Jeremiah, Jacks Dad and ran to his arms, quickly she was whisked with no words to the safety of the Hall, Agnes carefully pulled her sleeves over her burning wrist and bracelet and decided like Belle once before, she would tell nothing of her journey to the Fort, only with Avia would she share her story, when they were safe. Agnes joined Avia and Jack in the kitchen Miss Bonneville squealed with joy when she saw Agnes and settled her down in the warmth and huddle of the kitchen, folk were kind and did not ask questions, they were just glad that they were both safe and seemingly unharmed, Agnes knew the questions would come though, for now she closed her eyes so thankful Avia was safe and with Jack, she was back in her beloved Hall with her dressmaking and Miss Avia, Miss Bonneville, Belle and Jack, she thought of Avoca and was glad she still could love her and feel no anger, she was sad like Avoca they could never be together, their worlds had grown apart by time, fate, magic and a lot of witch trickery.

A FAMILY OCCASION
1811

Agnes and Avia often talked about their night of terror they did not share what they knew with anyone else though, Avia even held back on telling Jack some parts of it, Agnes's journey to the Fort Of Chitrakut was to much for many to believe and her burning bracelet and Preeti, Avia was completely intrigued though and wished she could meet Preeti one day she sounded wonderful, Agnes teased maybe one day she would take Avia on All Hallows Eve, they both wished this could happen. Both girls recovered well and people stopped asking about their ordeal. Avia's Father of course would be furious and hunts were sent out regularly for any who matched Agnes's and Avia's poor descriptions of their kidnappers. The story would travel and England became very unsafe for any witch, although they would not have witch hunts and trials like there used to be, other excuses would be used to persecute anyone who held anything that slightly resembled pagan beliefs or witch craft. The seasons had passed quickly and with them Agnes experienced a Christmas like no other, embraced by Avia's family, she spent the day as a lady and was treated to a feast unimaginable for a poor witch who came from 1408. The cold winter bought ice skating on the lake with furs and cloaks, Agnes took pity on the ice boy called Rudy he had a hard life stacking the cut ice from the lake in the huge bowl of stone and straw in the ice house, she would often take him extra food and made him promise on his Mother's life not to breath a word, she would tell him to have a little nap in the warm furs and Agnes would set to work with magic all the ice would be neatly stacked, giving little Rudy days to play and explore. Her dress's often were made in magical ways, her work was so was outstanding she became the most sought after seamstress in the land. Agnes never took for granted plentiful food and a warm room and bed, she had heard servants in other stately households were not so well looked after, with freezing rooms, little food and a meagre wage, Stourton though was as Jack had once said, the best household in the whole of England.

Agnes still saw Jack and Avia they seemed always to be together in the garden, Avia and Agnes would often have secret sleep overs in Avia's roomy chamber and they would chatter the night away, one such night Avia told Agnes exciting news that her sister Cecilia was to marry George and there was to be the grandest wedding for years at Stourton hall. Agnes was very excited, knowing full well she would be the lucky seamstress to design and make the special bridal gown, Avia and Agnes though agreed they did not want to marry, although Avia sighed as she said it and she told Agnes her secret, that she would marry Jack but knew they would never be aloud to, he was low born and she aristocracy never the twain should meet. Agnes felt sad for them she saw how dear they were to each other and Agnes without a word muddled this over in her mind, she was a witch surely she could do something to help her dearest friends. The months leading up to the wedding were full of excitement, there were parties for the engagement, parties for the families of the bride and groom to be and for the friends and acquaintances. The Hall was forever busy never had so many visitors wandered around the gardens, Avia could not wait for the wedding to pass and the tranquillity to resume to the gardens. She had not visited the Gothic cottage and garden since the night of All Hallows Eve, she was still scared that some spirit may catch her breath or a witch appear, she often thought of how petrifying the night had been and although Agnes bought the coven to her door, as Jack had feared, she also saved her and remained her protector for ever more. Avia believed Agnes would stay here and weave her magic forever, Avia had watched her once at work with a dress and she laughed in amazement at how such a spectacle created the most wondrous gowns. Agnes would stay until she could no more, for how long did a witch live for. Avia was excited for her sisters wedding and was dutiful in her kind remarks and pretence at her pleasure for her sister, whilst really she would rather she stayed at Stourton, Petworth was so faraway and she would miss her calming ways, Olivia would also become demanding taking her precious times with Jack, Avia knew though she must do as she was supposed to, to keep her freedom and of that she had far more than any other young girl did in her position. When eventually the grand day arrived Avia was thrilled the sun sparkled and the pretty June flowers swayed in a sweet scented wind. In their very finest they went in the carriage's to the beautiful little church in the grounds, St Peters was both part of the Hall and village so villagers crowded along the lane watching, the distinctive guests arrived it was a show of wealth and all stood in awe. Avia arrived at the church early with her sister and other relatives they stood at the front, Avia like her sister wore a delicate pale yellow dress with white flowers and lace, Agnes said they were like little daisy's dancing in the meadow, Avia tried to peer around at as many guests arrivals as she could, Olivia gave a little nervous cough and went quite flushed when Thomas and Edwina and their respected family arrived. The church was packed and some lesser guests filled the back. Avia turned to see Belle, Jeremiah, Bertie and Jack in the crowd she was shocked they had been invited and over whelmed with joy, she gave Jack an obvious huge wave to welcome him, he grinned in acknowledgement not daring to wave back. The music played and Cecilia entered the church with her Father who stood proudly by her side, Olivia and Avia looked at one another and knew each thought it would have been lovely for Mother to have seen. Miss Bonneville glowed and caught their eyes as she also understood and reassured them in some way. Avia was surprised how simple it seemed to marry, the service did not go on for ages, it was quite quick, soon they were all gathered outside and a procession of carriages took the bride and groom and guests to the Hall were the banquet began, Avia became pleased the service was short for the meal part took forever followed by dancing, she felt dizzy from punch and was glad to have Jack by her side, later some of the servants joined in including Agnes who looked stunning in her unusual red gown. Avia finally got chance to speak with Jack and he said tomorrow they must meet he had some exciting news to tell her that for now he must keep a secret.

ISABELLA MARIA DE BOURBON

A week before Cecilia's wedding to George from Petworth, Avia's father Lord Richard Hoare would invite Belle and her husband and their sons to an informal meeting in the huge library, a place he often liked to hold meetings, full of wonderful artefacts and art, he could enjoy showing his treasures whilst mixing business, it was a very wealthy time for his family profits soared in from their banking and property empire and his gold grew. He had also recently by inheritance acquired the properties of the late Lord Becklesford, his cousin who had no other family or heirs, not ever wishing to have children or marry. The Lord Becklesford had been the cousin, who had callously sent Belle to his Hall with no information of her link to French aristocracy, or any clue of who the poor mite was. Lord Richard had decided to gift Belle some of the inheritance, he also had news from France, he had applied for her birth rights and money still in her families name, during a short and hopeful restoration of royalty and aristocracy in France, Belle's link to aristocracy was on paper and she was the benefactor of a substantial wealth that had been held for her family, Lord Richard knew that Belle's husband would be shocked but he offered them considerable comfort and the opportunity to acquire Bonham Manor House, that had recently come available, they would still be able to work the farm which land ran along side the manors, they were also able to legally take Belle's name of aristocracy with royal ties, her full name was Isabella Maria De Bourbon. Belle of course understood she had known her secret for years, her poor husband and son Bertie though had no clue, yet Jack he seemed to find this no surprise and other than his thick Somerset drawl, he always had felt some sort of importance which allowed him to talk freely with opinion. Avia's Father asked him to stay behind after Belle, Jeremiah and Bertie had left with hand shakes and kisses. Lord Richard said he feared it would be hard for him now to be a garden labourer under his employment, Lord Richard however immediately unrolled some papers of plans he had and asked if perhaps Jack would consider being employed to help with the design and planting of his projects, with his daughter Avia's approval. Jack felt like jumping for joy instead he remained composed and accepted in the most polite manner he knew. Jack held all this secret, as the rest of the family did not want to cause a stir before Cecilia's wedding. Belle was delighted and was surprised how well her husband had taken the news. So the family planned to move to the manor and Belle would have as many dress's as she desired, Jeremiah said he always knew she was something special and instead of a hurt pride, he quite took to being Lord of his manor, although he would always be Jeremiah Feld once of the sheep glade.

BELLE'S HYPOTHESIS

Bella thought to herself often about Agnes and the witches and all that had happened, she wondered if it had not been for the witches and Jeremiah saving her in the woods, long ago on that All Hallows Eve and the Lord Richard Hoare being so pleased with Jack for saving his daughter and Agnes, that maybe none of this would have come about, something about it all made her think of Miss Bonneville and how well she had always treated her even as a servant, as if she some how knew she was aristocracy, it was a little like the way Miss Bonneville had taken Agnes so quickly with no hesitation, did she know something and she thought of Miss Bonneville and how she never looked any older and how she always knew things before they happened, she ran the strictest, yet happiest well treated household in England. Belle remembered back to the night she was taken by the witches and the way Miss Bonneville knew how to help her, she gave her a drink she had never tasted before, was that what she gave Avia and Agnes. Miss Bonneville always wore that pendant just like the one Miss Avia always strangely now wore. Belle asked herself the question, as she looked at her herbs she had been gifted by Miss Bonneville, she had taught her how to grind the seeds and mix the leaves, Rosemary for pain, Peppermint for colds, Sage for sore throats, Oregano for a boast of energy, Thyme and Basil for healing and other remedies and recipe. Miss Bonneville was certainly an extraordinary character and Belle just wondered knowing Agnes was a witch with such kindness and elegance, could Miss Bonville be a witch too. The more she thought the more similar they seemed, quick, intelligent and always a little ahead of everyone, yet not obviously, they both kept strange pets, Belle often noticed where ever Miss Bonneville was the magpie would follow and Agnes had that strange wild looking cat that appeared from nowhere and not many noticed, so sleek and allusive. Belle thought of so many things, a scratch or a sore were no more when you visited Miss Bonneville and any servants trouble from another was sorted with no word, she remembered how chores could disappear and sparkling glass and crockery shine like mirrors, the herbs and vegetable kitchen garden grew like no other at all times of year, admired by the cook though not noticed by many. Belle thought of Miss Bonneville and the stories she could tell and knowledge that she held. Belle had no proof it was her own secret theory, she felt quite certain though her friend Miss Bonneville was a witch of the highest calibre if such things existed, she wondered how much of their lives at Stourton Hall had prospered and bloomed with the loveliest witch of all.

THE SURPRISING THING ABOUT MISS BONNEVILLE

Miss Bonneville arrived at Stourton Hall quite by accident she blew in on an Autumn wind on All Hallows Eve and some mix up of her unexpected arrival extended to an interview with Lord Richard Hoare, for the position as a new housekeeper, a succession of applicants had applied and arrived and gone, none were quite what he was looking for, he needed someone he could trust to run a house and arrange social occasions at the beautiful Hall and gardens. Miss Bonneville had every answer and so much knowledge, she even had some understanding of his work in archeology and antiquities, above all she seemed kind, fare and strict with high morals almost from another time, she was both immaculate and articulate. Lord Richard employed her immediately and from that day on, the Hall seemed to have a bustle again, flowers filled the rooms, fires were lit, amazing food was served, delicate decor changes were made, his lovely wife Beatrice was enchanted and more than happy with her new housekeeper. While Miss Bonneville was in charge he was free to work and travel as he pleased. He did not ever feel the need to ask Miss Bonneville her christian name or where she had come from, she was so assertive and confident in her manner it seemed an unnecessary need; had he of asked her though, she would have most probably answered Mari and she would have said that she came from Normandy in France. Miss Bonneville was not really sure of her christian name she was born so long ago and had travelled far with her old family, They lived a simple life her Pa stole by night and her Ma sold herbs in the day, they lived in the woods and fields, she faintly remembered her parents, sister and brother with their wavy curls and freckles, unlike her dark tight ringlets and flawless complexion, they were stocky and stout while she was tall and slender, Miss Bonneville remembered kindness and love, all so long ago she tried not to think of her own loss and theirs. One stormy day they fell upon a chateau and her Pa asked for shelter for the night in exchange for some work on the land, the owner of the chateau had a face like thunder himself and scared the children so they hid, they slept in the huge barn and stayed for longer than one night, they worked hard by day and were fed well with a roof over their heads each night, the children grew less fearful and were enticed by the strange owners pretty black kittens, they played in his gardens and watched his magical fire displays, the days seemed kind and they did not choose to move on. Sadly though all good things must come to an end and one day the strange owner bid them farewell, he offered them a purse of gold and a cart and horse in exchange for their eldest daughter. He promised he would school her and her life would be rich and free, that was the day they were all tricked and she was captured. She was kept by the strange owner who was a warlock, in truth he gave her great knowledge, freedom though was something she would forget, his remote Chateau de le Angotiere was a perfect spot with no passers bye or questions. At the chateau he could create his firework displays and explosives. The warlock had studied in ancient China to gain his gun powder skills, he sold the gun powder to who ever was in need for the highest price, be it the French or the English both were always in need with the hundred year war just starting to rage on, the year was 1337 so it had only just begun. Miss Bonneville realised she had been taken for a reason, he had watched her when her family lived there and she was snatched because she was special, the warlock told her she was a supreme witch born under a dark black moon and this was her calling to stay with him. He trained her in both magic and management and she became his apprentice and spy, no one paid attention to a young girl, as she grew he used her beauty as an enticement to further his connections, he would call her Miss Bonneville, she did not count how many years she spent in his service to escape was futile, although he was strange and dark in his ways, the warlock called Fabian was respectful and kind to her in many ways and he taught her more than any person could ever hope to know, life went on for Miss Bonneville in this way for an eternity. Fabian had many witches and warlocks visit him over the years, some she remembered well and some she liked better than others, the arrival of a witch named Martiale Espaze who weaved her path one winters day through the warlocks door, was the undoing of his long success, Miss Bonneville warned him she was evil to the core, her trial of horrors for witch craft and worse, dragged the warlock to the attention of others and the publicity of her execution, gave the warlock Fabian only one choice and that was to evanesce without a trace. Without a word to Miss Bonneville he disappeared and she was free, the law of the land searched the chateau and found gun powders and more. Miss Bonneville was under no suspicion though and she told them of her long capture and with pity was let go, with papers in her hand and money in her purse Miss Bonneville was gone.

THE HIRING OF
NANNY MAUD

Another strange and very small thing that Miss Bonneville also had to consider, with witches flying wild in the skies, was dear Nanny Maud. Hence her bad fever on All Hallows Eve each year. This indeed was a perilous time for her and should she be spotted by a passing bad tempered witch it would sadly be game over for her. Previously Miss Bonneville had interviewed so many useless nannies it had become impossible, no one fitted the description the Lord asked for, it was unachievable to find a single person with all those attributes. So Miss Bonneville took it upon herself to fill the gap in an alternative manner. She had watched the little mouse Maud she kept as a pet, so sweet and observant a clever little mouse, who was trained so well, she knew the house, the children, the history and how things worked, so for a well needed temporary fix on a still summers eve, the spell was cast and Nanny Maud appeared, at first a little muddled she worked hard and by morning was a shy and quiet little lady, by lunch time her tail had fallen and by the next day she was elementary and improving by the hour, Miss Bonneville was content and slightly smug with her creation and Nanny Maud was put with the children, who instantly adored her, even Miss Bonneville could never had expected the shear wonder of the mouse, a perfect natural in the nursery and devoted to the core, Nanny Maud would stay for a very long time, for a temporary fix.

FABIAN BENZLASTIEN
1809

Lord Richard Hoare was in full swing of the summer of 1809 he had yet another year of profits and invested his time in travels and archaeology on such a dig took him to the foothills of Nepal, here he would make acquaintance with a Russian explorer and although it was not customary for conversation with a man who's countries were not allies with France, the two men had a toxic wealth of knowledge and were intrigued by each others explorations and excavations, Fabian had the rare opportunity of a trip to London and asked if he might be able to visit Stourton Hall and its famous gardens. On a cold winters evening on All Hallows Eve Fabian arrived for dinner at Stourton Hall he was amongst a number of guests, Lord Richard on reflection felt uneasy about spending time with a strange explorer alone. The guests were well entertained with fireworks a gift from Fabian and by the light of fires and candles they all had a spectacular evening tour of the gardens. Miss Bonneville immediately recognised Fabian no one else in the world had such deep dark eyes and heavy black eyebrows, his face told stories with no words, she felt a tremor of fear, he ignored her presence though and looked through her as though she did not exist, Miss Bonneville returned the favour, she however could not think what an earth he was doing here and what he was up to, twice she saw him sneaking to different parts of the house pretending to be lost and whilst on the garden tour he hesitated for so long outside the Gothic cottage, Miss Bonneville watched him from a far he was up to something and even on that night Miss

Bonneville knew he had something to do with Belle's witches, she had seen them herself at different times in the woods and she remembered them well as visitors to the chateau. So now it all made perfect sense he had come to set his spells making way for the witches entrance, he knew Agnes was by the cottage all that time and the short dumpy witch with freckles and a ridiculous amount of dress's on, had been seen around the woods all year, no doubt spying and informing. After Miss Bonneville had seen Fabian that night in her safe hold at Stourton Hall, she had had a busy time setting her own defences, she had already made sure that the moonstone was placed in Avia's possession, nervous of her playing by the Gothic cottage, afraid Avia was now entwined into the story, she would then set a deflection spell by the witches portal sending them off course, she would set little protection spells all over the grounds, the annoying witch she now knew was Lettice she would set a spy on. Nothing was more easily trained and compliant than a chatterpie, commonly known as a magpie, these annoying raucous birds were a wonderful witches pet, poor Hex as she named him was caught up in one of Otto the gamekeepers traps, she fed him well on scraps and within a week he was hers, Hex would arrive dutifully for his breakfast early and be lead to the wood choppers hut where Lettice hid, Hex would soon fly to Lettice and sit close by in hope of scraps, Lettice obliged well, as Miss Bonneville knew she would and all day and night Hex would follow and watch, Hex would then fly back to his true mistress Miss Bonneville, she saw everything through his eyes, she saw Lettice spy on the strange little girl who had suddenly appeared and played with Avia and Jack. Miss Bonneville was reminded of someone vividly when she saw the strange girl with the shiny black hair and when Miss Bonnevillle saw Agnes at Belle's market stall, she knew it was a set up and she played along well and as soon as she saw Agnes close up, she knew straight away without doubt this was Avoca's daughter the little witch of a warlock to be sacrificed, she remembered now the witches so clearly all so beautiful and charming, she heard their plotting with the warlock Fabian at the chateau, when Avoca was distracted by the little black kittens or fast a sleep from the witches potions, Miss Bonneville had tried to warn her once or twice that her friends meant her harm, the witches and warlock were clever though and she was given no chance to ever do so. Now all these years on she stood next to the daughter, with the knowledge that she was in grave danger. Little Miss Avia and Belle had created a perfect plot, she could now keep the girl Agnes safe with her in the Hall, with the added bonus she seemed to truly be a perfect seamstress.

Miss Bonneville though had underestimated the powers and cunningness of the witches and warlock, they managed to still find there way back to Stourton with ease and into the Hall, she was powerless that night it all happened so fast, Miss Bonneville felt dreadful, with thanks to Jack though Avia was saved and Miss Bonneville was sure Avoca had somehow saved her daughter, one day she would love to have a little chat with her and hear her story. For now though Miss Bonneville felt a small glisten of satisfaction, she did not believe the witches or warlock were strong enough to come back for a good few hundred years if ever and she would protect Stourton when they did return. For now though she could enjoy her place in peace and Hex she would keep he was very useful, he sat outside her office in the tree watching the gardens, Miss Bonville saw no harm in having a permanent pet and spy in such times.

FOUR CROSS WITCHES AND A WARLOCK 1669

Tricked, banished and nearly burned at the stake, the witches managed to return to the quiet house by the lake were Parnell and Wilmot always wished to begin their favourite year 1650 when all was quiet and still, they were all weakened by their failing to not sacrifice the witches and warlocks child, they did not have strength to even complain, Lettice would become ill and wither away her time on the earth had been so long, the others though would struggle on and find other less successful sacrifices to keep them alive, the witches of Siljan Lake had stayed tucked away for hundreds of years, in their desperation though to stay strong and alive, they had grown careless with their prey and the city people of Mora started to talk and grew suspicious of children's encounters in the woods, what once had been folk lore and stories became an investigation of missing children and animals over the years and with talk of witches, Mora started the witch hunt and not many would slip the net, the trials were brutal and many innocent would be accused. Josina, Wilmot, Parnell and Fabian were all eventually captured unaware and found guilty, one though would mysteriously disappear from capture and never be found. The others would be hung quietly one cold winters night, the ice on the lake reflected the rising moon and a phenomena of coloured lights was seen as never before, it was told the spirits danced in the skies to celebrate the passing of evil and peace on earth.

PRINCE & FROG

Belle loved her new home and wandered the rooms often with her friends, Miss Avia, Agnes and Miss Bonneville who after all theses years asked to be called Mari, all entwined by the witches they had a bond and enjoyed each others company greatly. Belle's family had taken to a good life well and the farm now prospered with extra land and a boost of labourers, Belle would pinch herself that all this had happened, Avia could be no more delighted than any one possible her garden labourer had over night turned out to be high born. Avia had found the house strange without Cecelia since her wedding and missed her, Olivia seemed to be always with Edwina plotting her own wedding day and life of comfort with Thomas, who was now studying in London. Lottie had now started working at the hall so she managed to catch up with her old friend, Avia also had her special Agnes, the little yew tree witch, who still worked hard and fixed little spells, their fellowship would always be. Jack and Avia worked on the garden plans and together they created wonderful ideas, they would spend hours walking through the fields and woods, Jack would joke he thought Miss Avia must have slipped him a quick kiss, because he the frog had turned into a prince. Stourton Hall felt safe and calm and Avia was the happiest she could ever be and knew she could spend her life wandering these gardens and rooms and keeping their beauty and splendour for other lives to see. Hopefully with Jack by her side laughter would always be close and friendship would last for eternity and the yew tree now blossomed with beautiful strange flowers instead of strange charms an amazing phenomenon many would see.

THE END

THE AUTHOR

Since a child I have written and drawn, my first book took me years to be brave enough to publish and I still feel nervous to share my work, I write for pleasure and love to research and bring places I have explored into my books, I am inspired by historical places and facts and my love of nature and art. I studied literature and art and worked in the world of fashion before I had my own family. I now work with autistic children as a support worker and write books. I hope you, the reader enjoy my books.

Other Books

The Revenge Of Merga Bein

Sally In The Woods

The Curate The Witch & The Casket

Tetonti & The Grand Quest

Dolly Mouse & Friends

COPYRIGHT

This is a fictional book © Written & Illustrated by Victoria J Hunt

First Published in May 2019

Some contents of this book contain historical events, names and places the information and dates may not be accurate and they have only been used in a fictional manner.